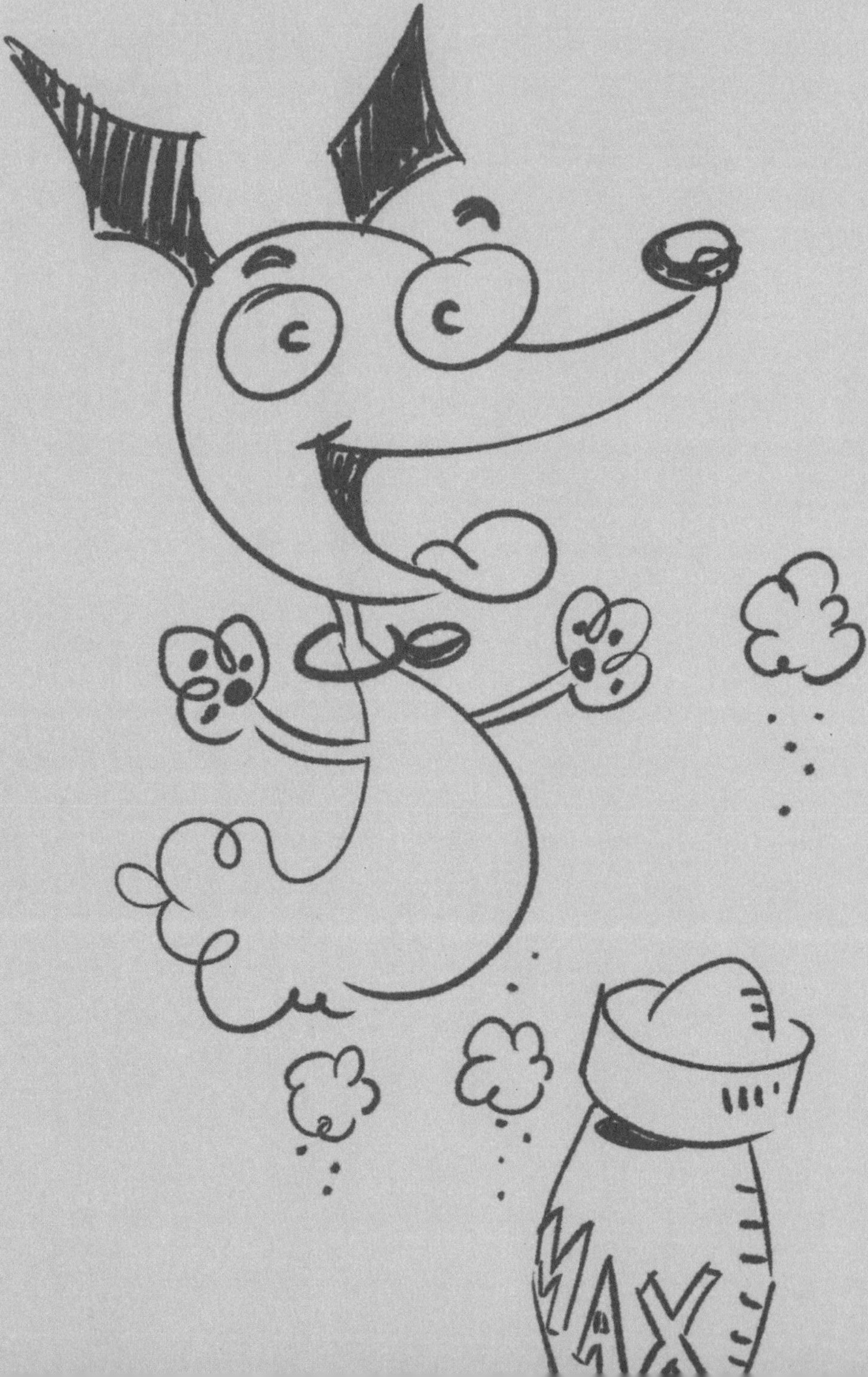
MAX

BULLY FOR YOU!

Down with CATS

FORGET Felines!

BAD KITTY!

By Dana Sullivan

RED CHAIR ·PRESS·

Egremont, Massachusetts

Dead Max Comix is produced and published by:

Red Chair Press   PO Box 333   South Egremont, MA 01258-0333

www.redchairpress.com

 FREE Discussion Guide at www.redchairpress.com/free-resources

To Vicki.
—Dana

Publisher's Cataloging-In-Publication Data

Names: Sullivan, Dana, 1958- author, illustrator. | Sullivan, Dana, 1958-Dead Max comix.
Title: Bully for you! / by Dana Sullivan.

Description: Egremont, Massachusetts : Red Chair Press, [2021] | Series: Dead Max comix ; book 3 | Interest age level: 009-014. | Summary: "Derrick finally feels like he's getting the hang of Middle School. He's in a band with his best friends and his dogs Bennie and Max are getting along. Even his Dead Max comics and advice columns are a hit, until Max's cat-hating ways start raising hackles with his cat-loving readers. Then when Derrick's cartoons protesting racism backfire, the Muslim kids turn against him and the paper is in danger of being shut down, along with Derrick's cartooning career. Is Derrick a racist bully or trying to help some friends fight hatred? Luckily, Dead Max and some fishy characters are on the case, sleuthing out the real culprit and reuniting the students of Zachary Taylor Middle School with some long, lost friends"-- Provided by publisher.

Identifiers: ISBN 9781634408646 (HC) | ISBN 9781634408653 (PB) | ISBN 9781634408660 (ebook)

Subjects: LCSH: Middle school students--Comic books, strips, etc. | Cartoonists--Comic books, strips, etc. | Racism--Comic books, strips, etc. | Bullies--Comic books, strips, etc. | CYAC: Middle school students--Fiction. | Cartoonists--Fiction. | Racism--Fiction. | Bullies--Fiction. | LCGFT: Graphic novels.

Classification: LCC PZ7.7.S853 Bul 2021 (print) | LCC PZ7.7.S853 (ebook) | DDC 741.5973 [Fic]--dc23

LC record available at https://lccn.loc.gov/2020937814

Text & Illustration copyright © 2021 Dana Sullivan
RED CHAIR PRESS, the RED CHAIR and associated logos are registered trademarks of Red Chair Press LLC.

Printed in the United States of America

0920 1P CGS21

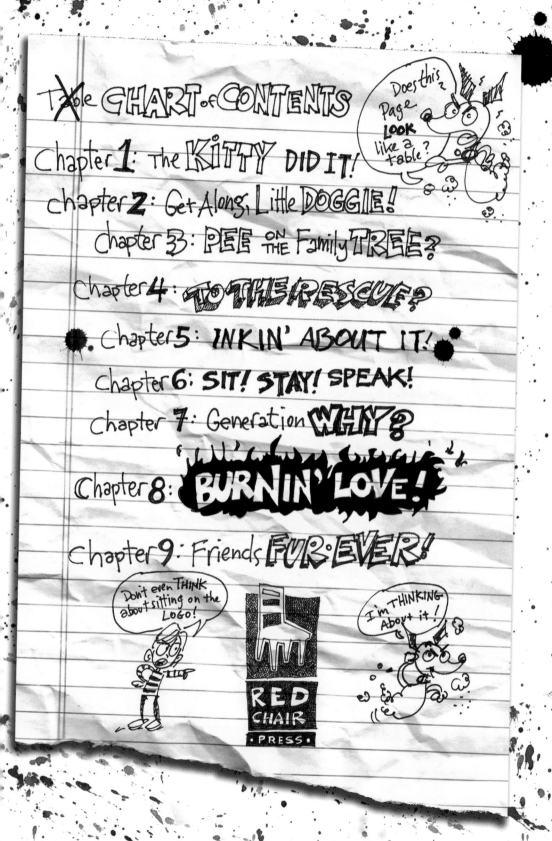

~~Table~~ CHART of CONTENTS

Does this Page LOOK like a table?

Don't even THINK about sitting on the LOGO!

RED CHAIR ·PRESS·

I'm THINKING About it!

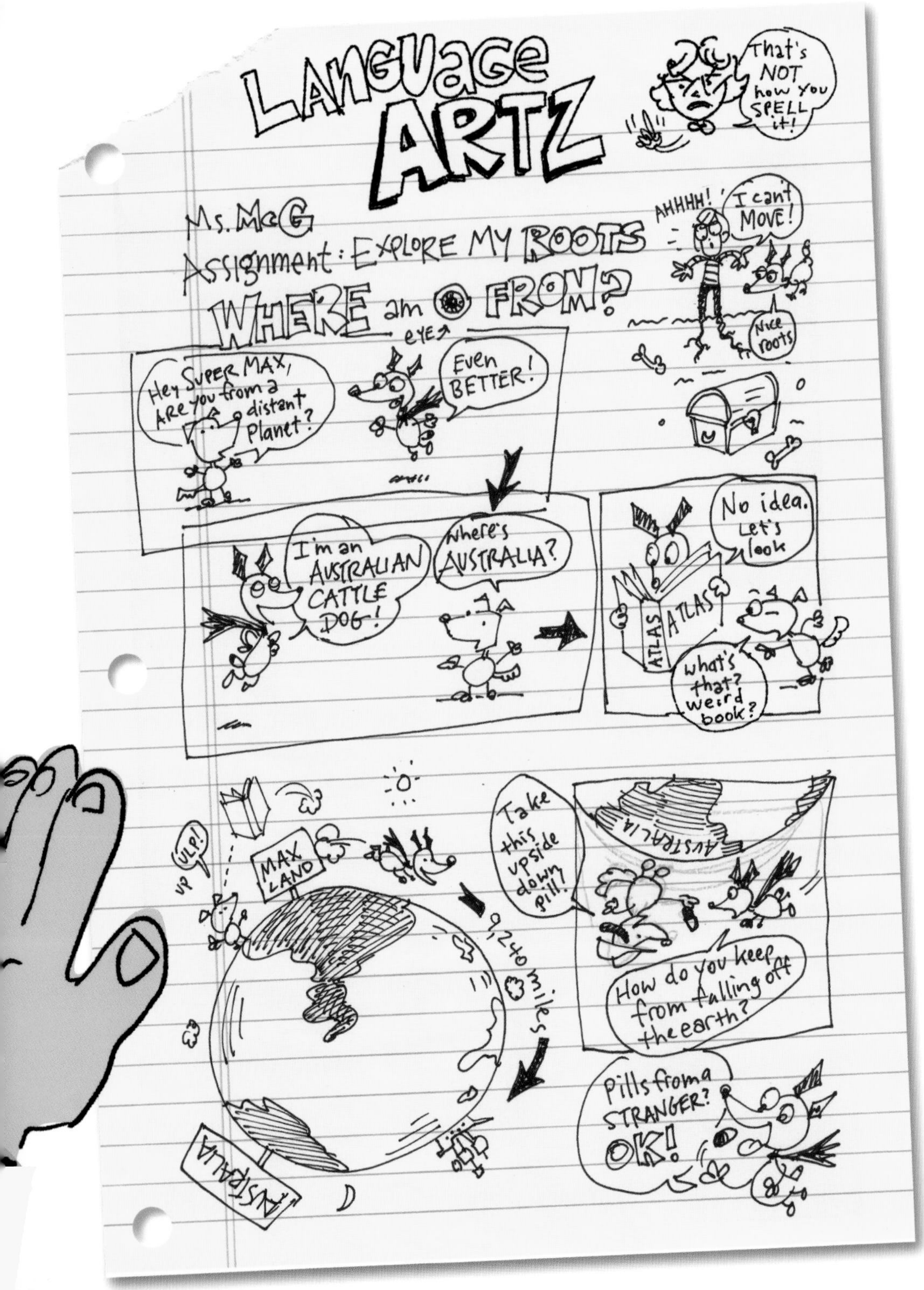
LANGUAGE ARTZ
That's NOT how you SPELL it!
Ms. McG
Assignment: EXPLORE MY ROOTS
WHERE am FROM?
eye
AHHHH!
I can't MOVE!
Nice roots
Hey SUPER MAX, are you from a distant Planet?
Even BETTER!
I'm an AUSTRALIAN CATTLE DOG!
Where's AUSTRALIA?
No idea. Let's look
ATLAS
ATLAS
what's that? weird book?
ULP!
UP
MAX LAND
9,240 miles
AUSTRALIA
Take this upside down pill!
AUSTRALIA
How do you keep from falling off the earth?
Pills from a STRANGER? OK!

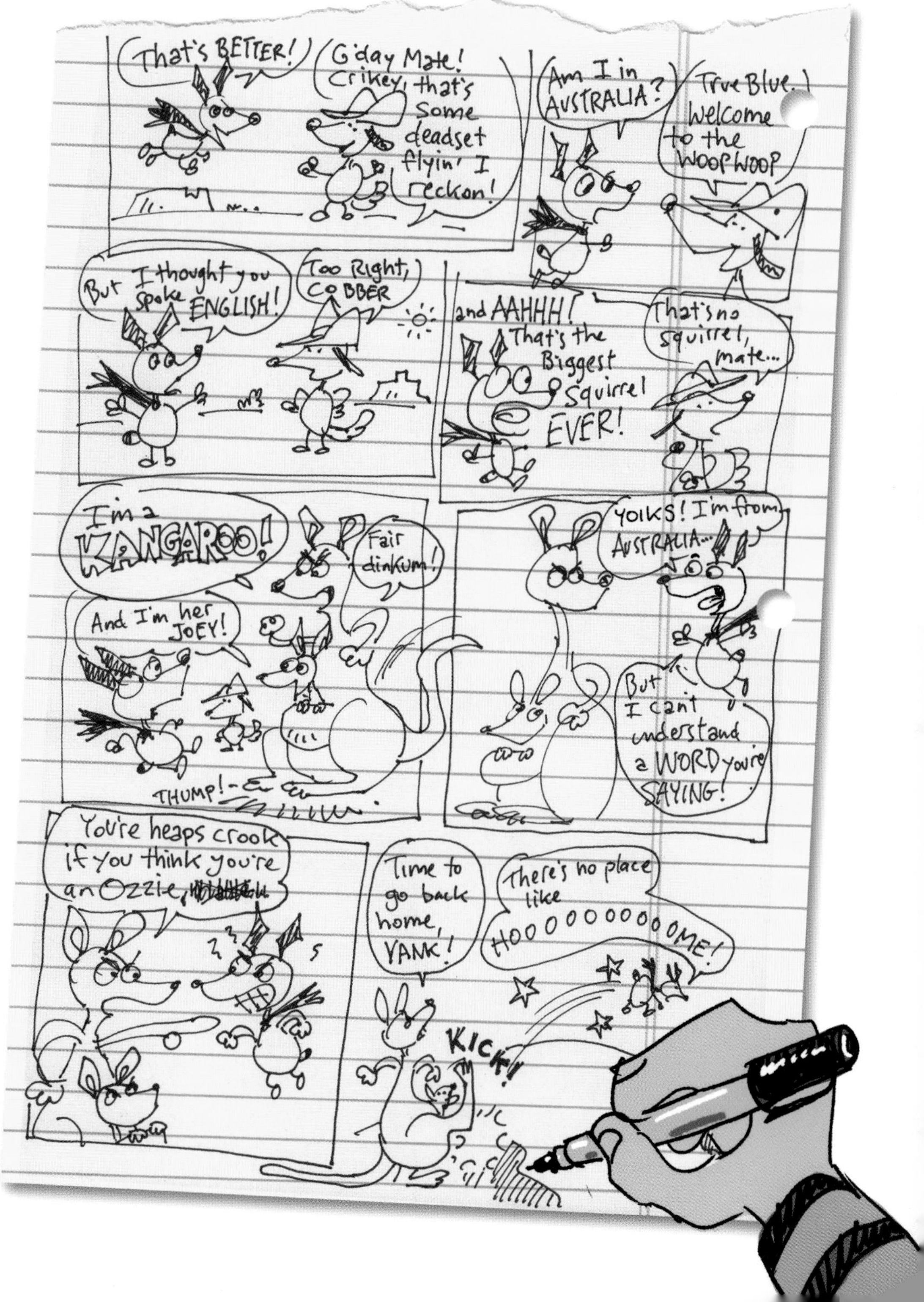
That's BETTER!
G'day Mate! Crikey, that's some deadset flyin' I reckon!
Am I in AUSTRALIA?
True Blue. Welcome to the WOOP WOOP
But I thought you spoke ENGLISH!
Too Right, COBBER
and AAHHH! That's the Biggest Squirrel EVER!
That's no squirrel, mate...
I'm a KANGAROO!
Fair dinkum!
And I'm her JOEY!
THUMP!
YOIKS! I'm from AUSTRALIA...
But I cant understand a WORD you're SAYING!
You're heaps crook if you think you're an Ozzie,
Time to go back home, YANK!
KICK!
There's no place like HOOOOOOOOOOME!

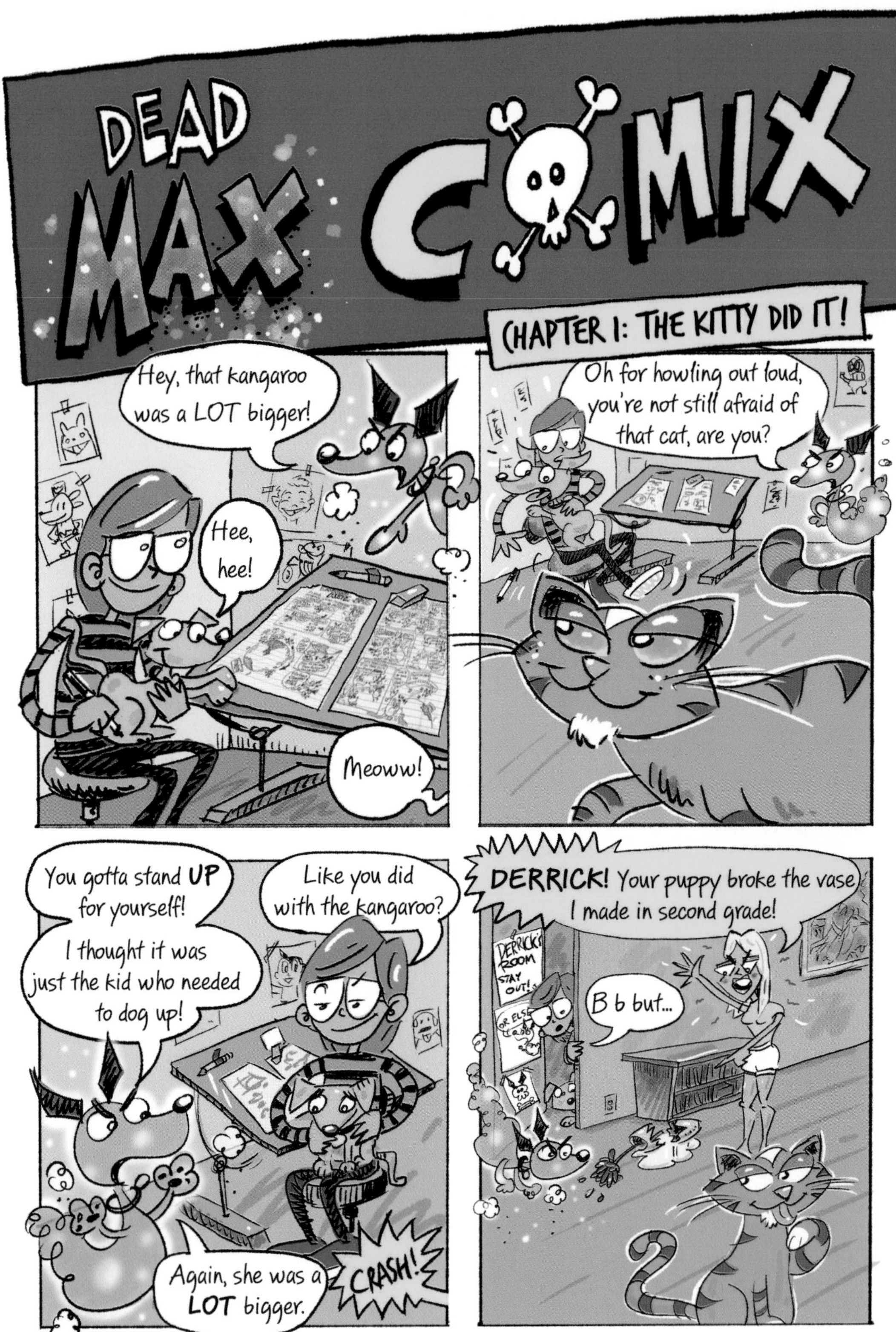
DEAD MAX COMIX
CHAPTER 1: THE KITTY DID IT!
Hey, that kangaroo was a LOT bigger!
Hee, hee!
Meoww!
Oh for howling out loud, you're not still afraid of that cat, are you?
You gotta stand UP for yourself!
Like you did with the kangaroo?
I thought it was just the kid who needed to dog up!
Again, she was a LOT bigger.
CRASH!
DERRICK! Your puppy broke the vase I made in second grade!
DERRICK'S ROOM STAY OUT!
OR ELSE
B b but...

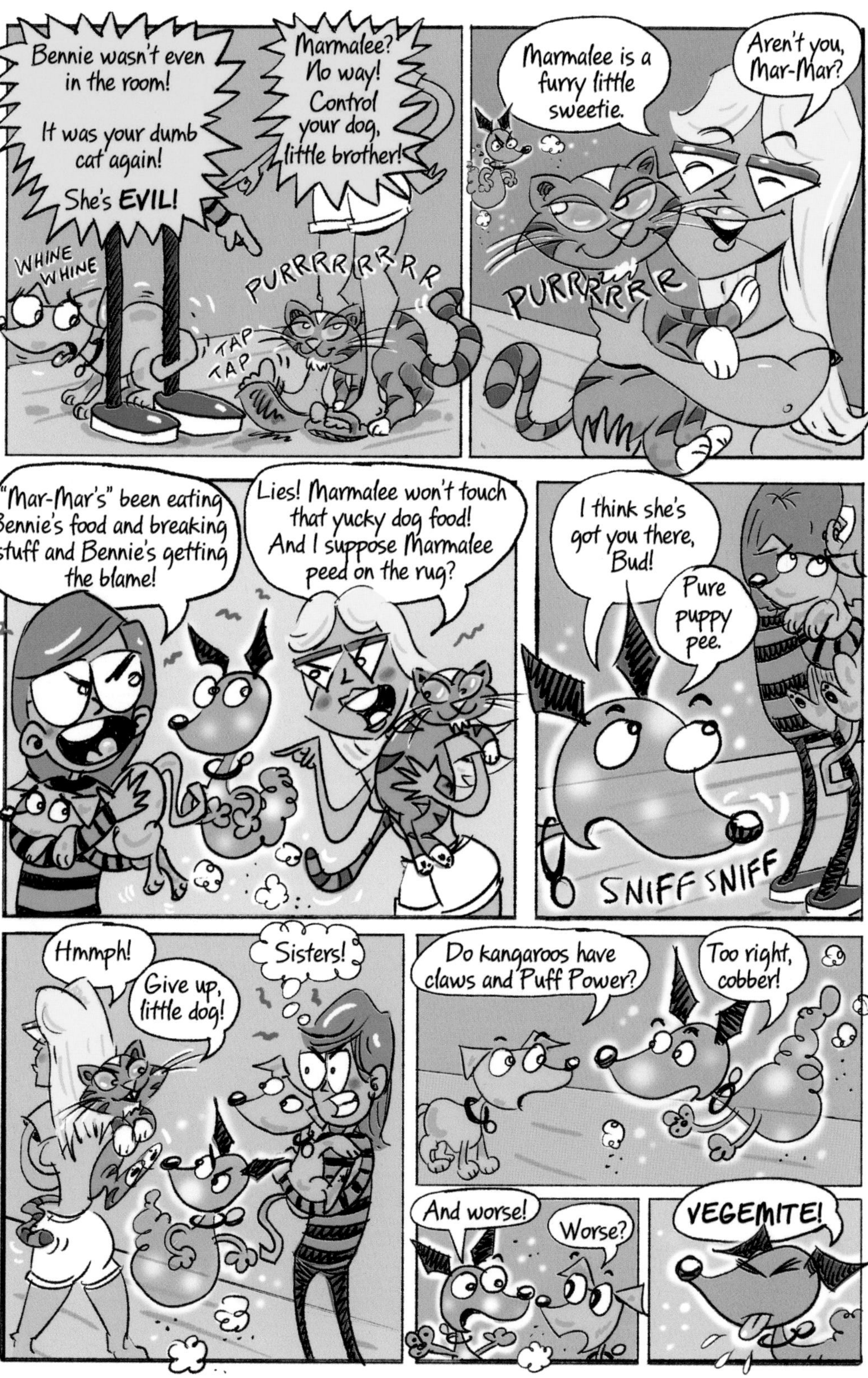
Bennie wasn't even in the room!
It was your dumb cat again!
She's **EVIL!**
Marmalee? No way! Control your dog, little brother!
WHINE WHINE
PURRRRRRRRR
TAP TAP
Marmalee is a furry little sweetie.
Aren't you, Mar-Mar?
PURRRRRR
"Mar-Mar's" been eating Bennie's food and breaking stuff and Bennie's getting the blame!
Lies! Marmalee won't touch that yucky dog food! And I suppose Marmalee peed on the rug?
I think she's got you there, Bud!
Pure puppy pee.
SNIFF SNIFF
Hmmph!
Give up, little dog!
Sisters!
Do kangaroos have claws and Puff Power?
Too right, cobber!
And worse!
Worse?
VEGEMITE!

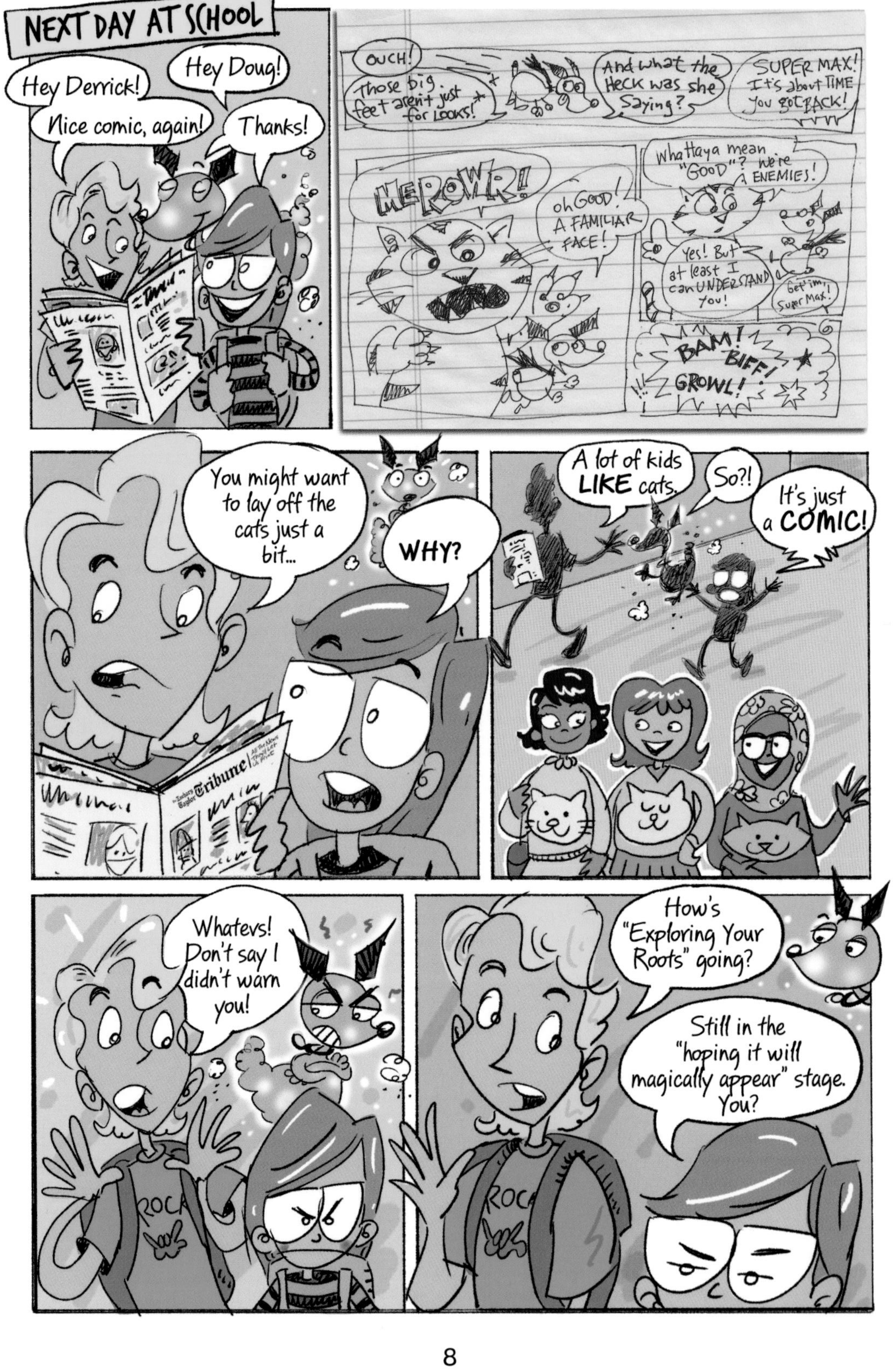

NEXT DAY AT SCHOOL
Hey Derrick!
Hey Doug!
Nice comic, again!
Thanks!
OUCH!
Those big feet aren't just for LOOKS!
And what the Heck was she Saying?
SUPER MAX! It's about TIME you got BACK!
MEROWR!
oh GOOD! A FAMILIAR FACE!
Whattaya mean "GOOD"? We're ENEMIES!
Yes! But at least I can UNDERSTAND you!
Get 'im, Super Max!
BAM! BIFF! GROWL!
You might want to lay off the cats just a bit...
WHY?
A lot of kids **LIKE** cats.
So?!
It's just a **COMIC!**
Whatevs! Don't say I didn't warn you!
How's "Exploring Your Roots" going?
Still in the "hoping it will magically appear" stage. You?

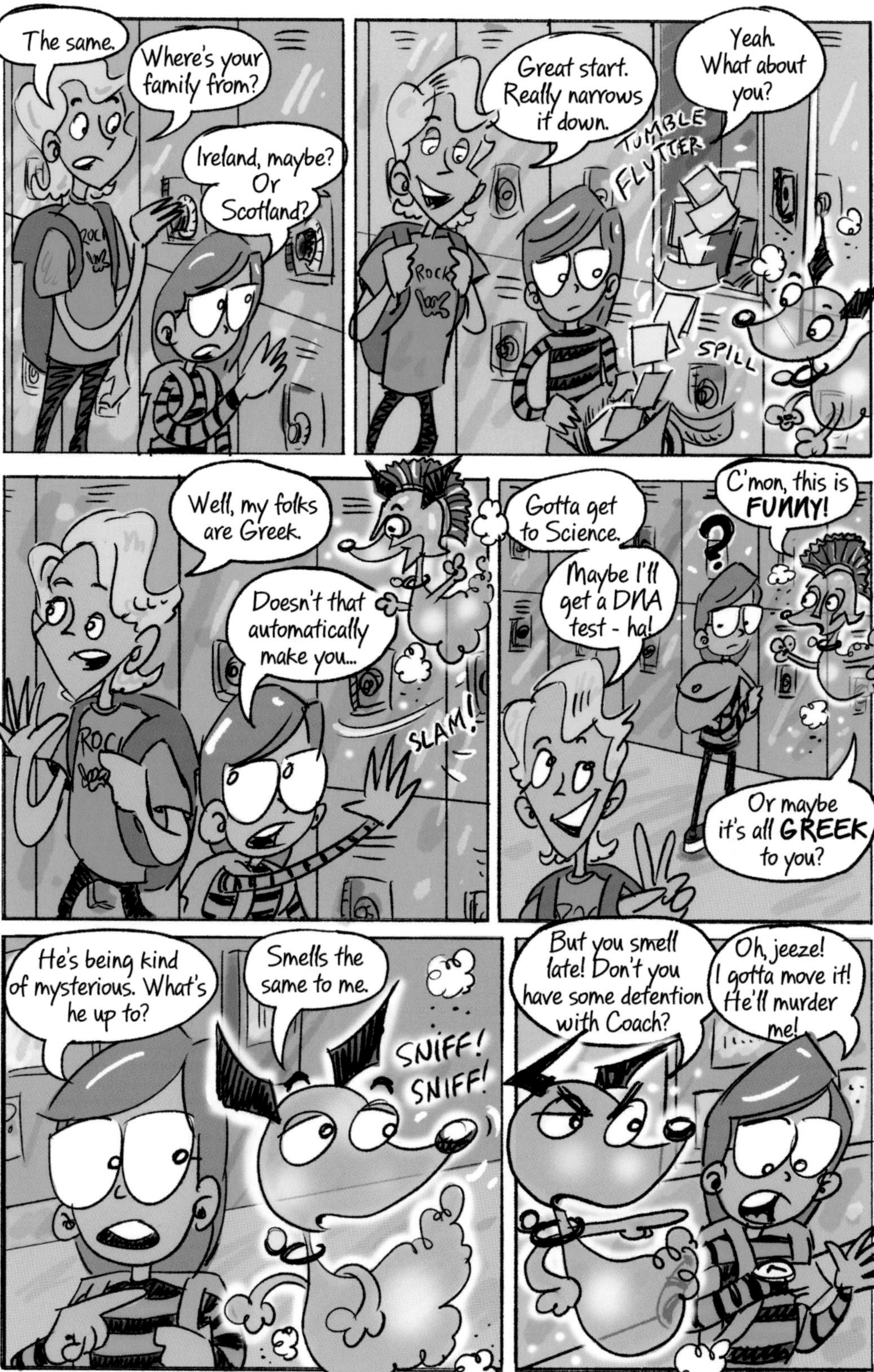
The same.
Where's your family from?
Ireland, maybe? Or Scotland?
Great start. Really narrows it down.
Yeah. What about you?
TUMBLE
FLUTTER
SPILL
Well, my folks are Greek.
Doesn't that automatically make you...
SLAM!
Gotta get to Science.
Maybe I'll get a DNA test - ha!
C'mon, this is FUNNY!
?
Or maybe it's all GREEK to you?
He's being kind of mysterious. What's he up to?
Smells the same to me.
SNIFF! SNIFF!
But you smell late! Don't you have some detention with Coach?
Oh, jeeze! I gotta move it! He'll murder me!

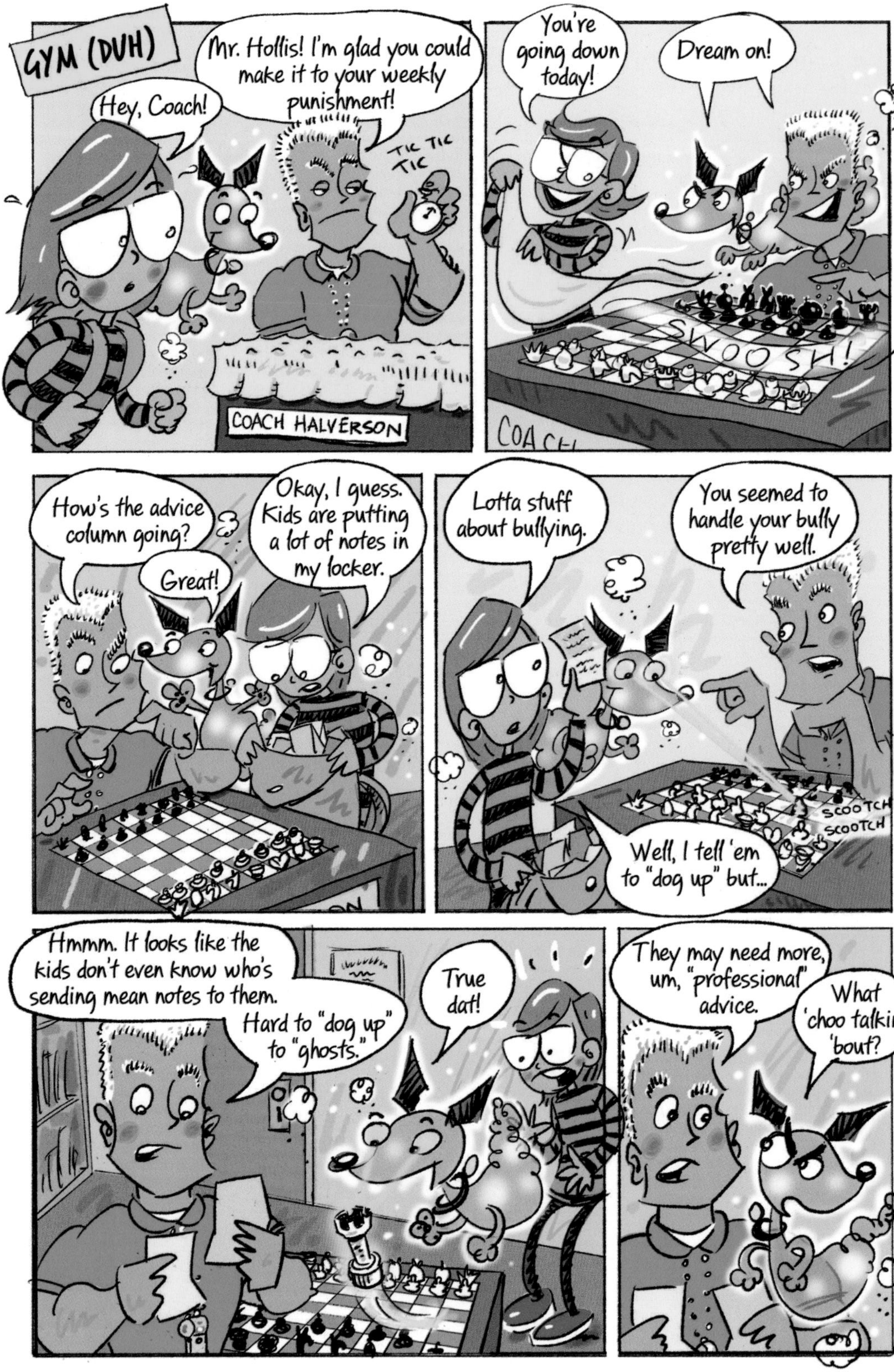
GYM (DUH)
Hey, Coach!
Mr. Hollis! I'm glad you could make it to your weekly punishment!
TIC TIC TIC
COACH HALVERSON
You're going down today!
Dream on!
SWOOSH!
COACH
How's the advice column going?
Great!
Okay, I guess. Kids are putting a lot of notes in my locker.
Lotta stuff about bullying.
You seemed to handle your bully pretty well.
SCOOTCH SCOOTCH
Well, I tell 'em to "dog up" but...
Hmmm. It looks like the kids don't even know who's sending mean notes to them.
Hard to "dog up" to "ghosts."
True dat!
They may need more, um, "professional" advice.
What 'choo talkin' 'bout?

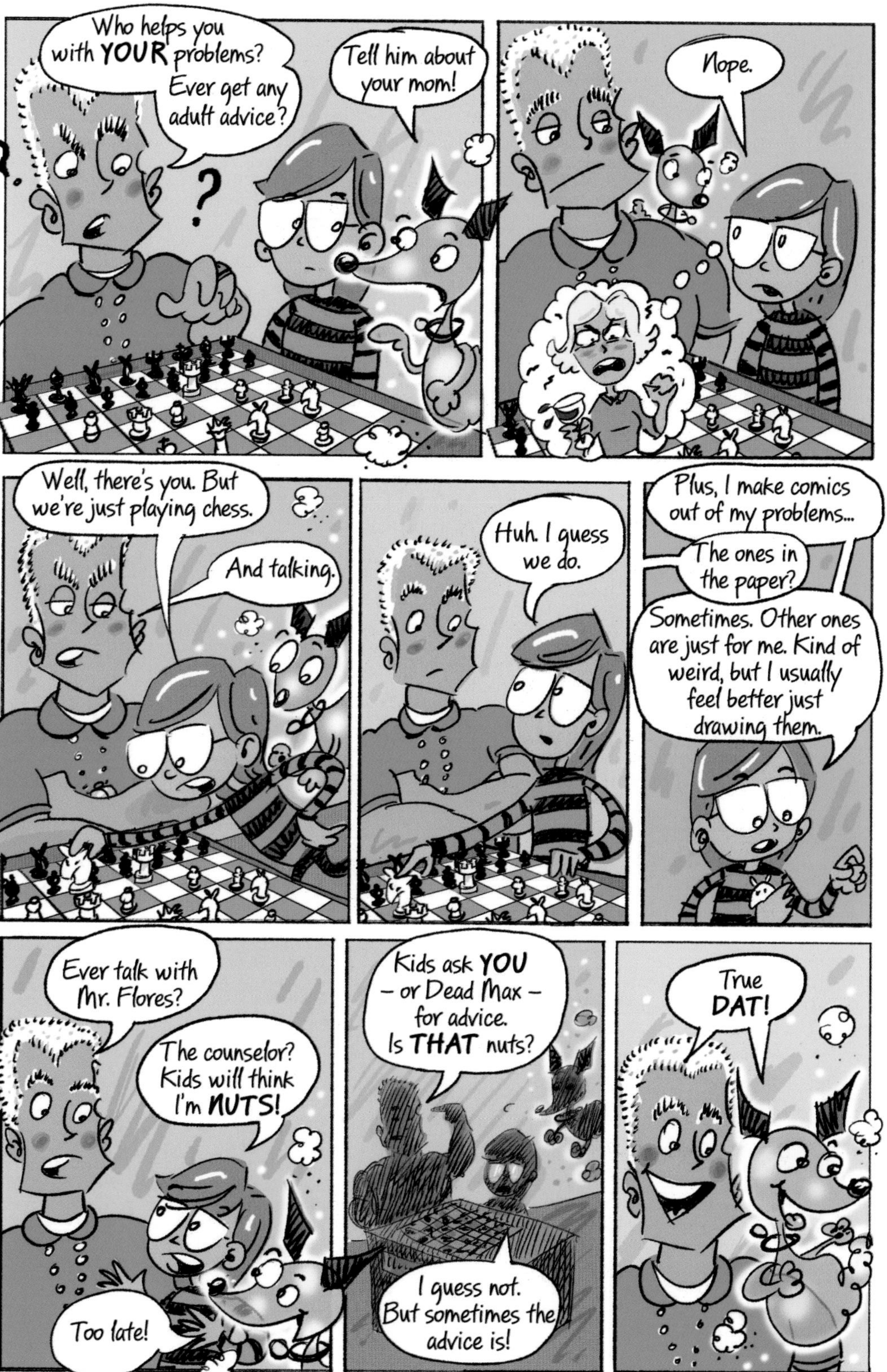
Who helps you with YOUR problems?
Ever get any adult advice?
Tell him about your mom!
Nope.
Well, there's you. But we're just playing chess.
And talking.
Huh. I guess we do.
Plus, I make comics out of my problems...
The ones in the paper?
Sometimes. Other ones are just for me. Kind of weird, but I usually feel better just drawing them.
Ever talk with Mr. Flores?
The counselor? Kids will think I'm NUTS!
Too late!
Kids ask YOU – or Dead Max – for advice. Is THAT nuts?
I guess not. But sometimes the advice is!
True DAT!

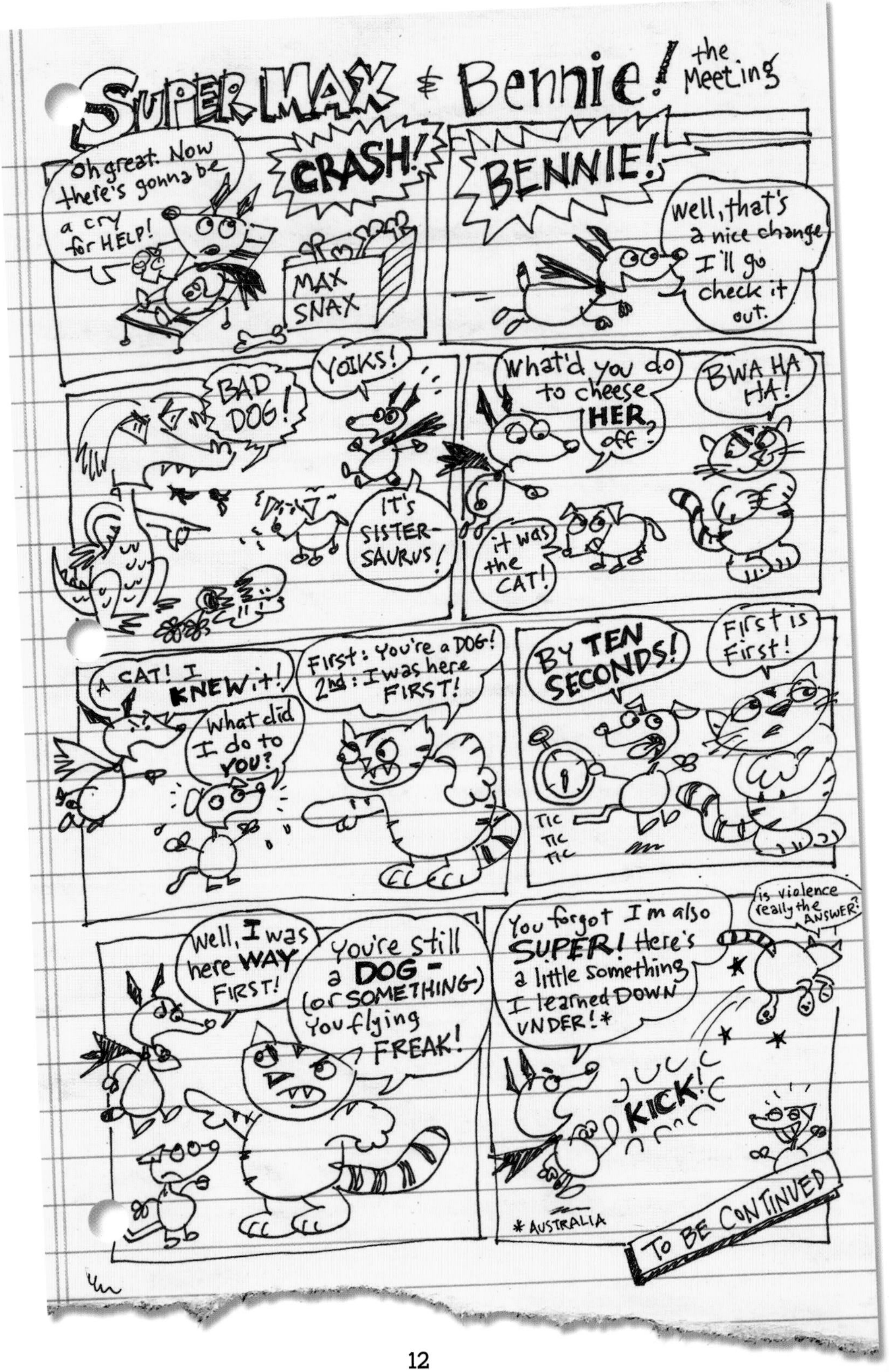
SUPER MAX & Bennie!
the Meeting
Oh great. Now there's gonna be a cry for HELP!
CRASH!
MAX SNAX
BENNIE!
Well, that's a nice change. I'll go check it out.
BAD DOG!
YOIKS!
It's SISTER-SAURUS!
What'd you do to cheese HER off?
BWA HA HA!
it was the CAT!
A CAT! I KNEW it!
What did I do to YOU?
First: You're a DOG! 2nd: I was here FIRST!
BY TEN SECONDS!
First is First!
TIC TIC TIC
Well, I was here WAY FIRST!
You're still a DOG - (or SOMETHING) You flying FREAK!
You forgot I'm also SUPER! Here's a little something I learned DOWN UNDER!*
is violence really the ANSWER?
KICK!
* AUSTRALIA
TO BE CONTINUED

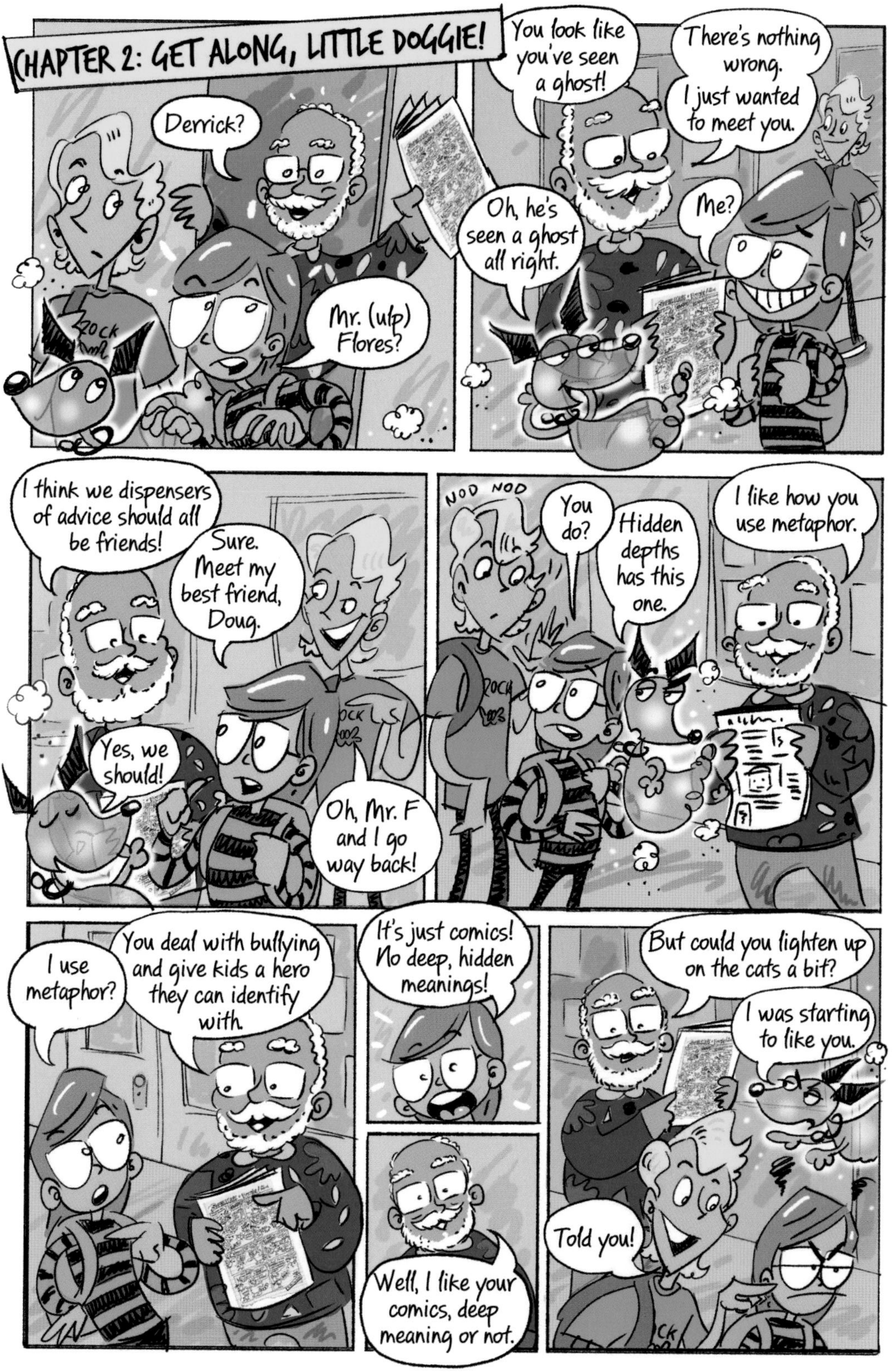
CHAPTER 2: GET ALONG, LITTLE DOGGIE!
Derrick?
Mr. (ulp) Flores?
You look like you've seen a ghost!
There's nothing wrong. I just wanted to meet you.
Me?
Oh, he's seen a ghost all right.
I think we dispensers of advice should all be friends!
Sure. Meet my best friend, Doug.
Yes, we should!
Oh, Mr. F and I go way back!
NOD NOD
You do?
Hidden depths has this one.
I like how you use metaphor.
I use metaphor?
You deal with bullying and give kids a hero they can identify with.
It's just comics! No deep, hidden meanings!
Well, I like your comics, deep meaning or not.
But could you lighten up on the cats a bit?
I was starting to like you.
Told you!

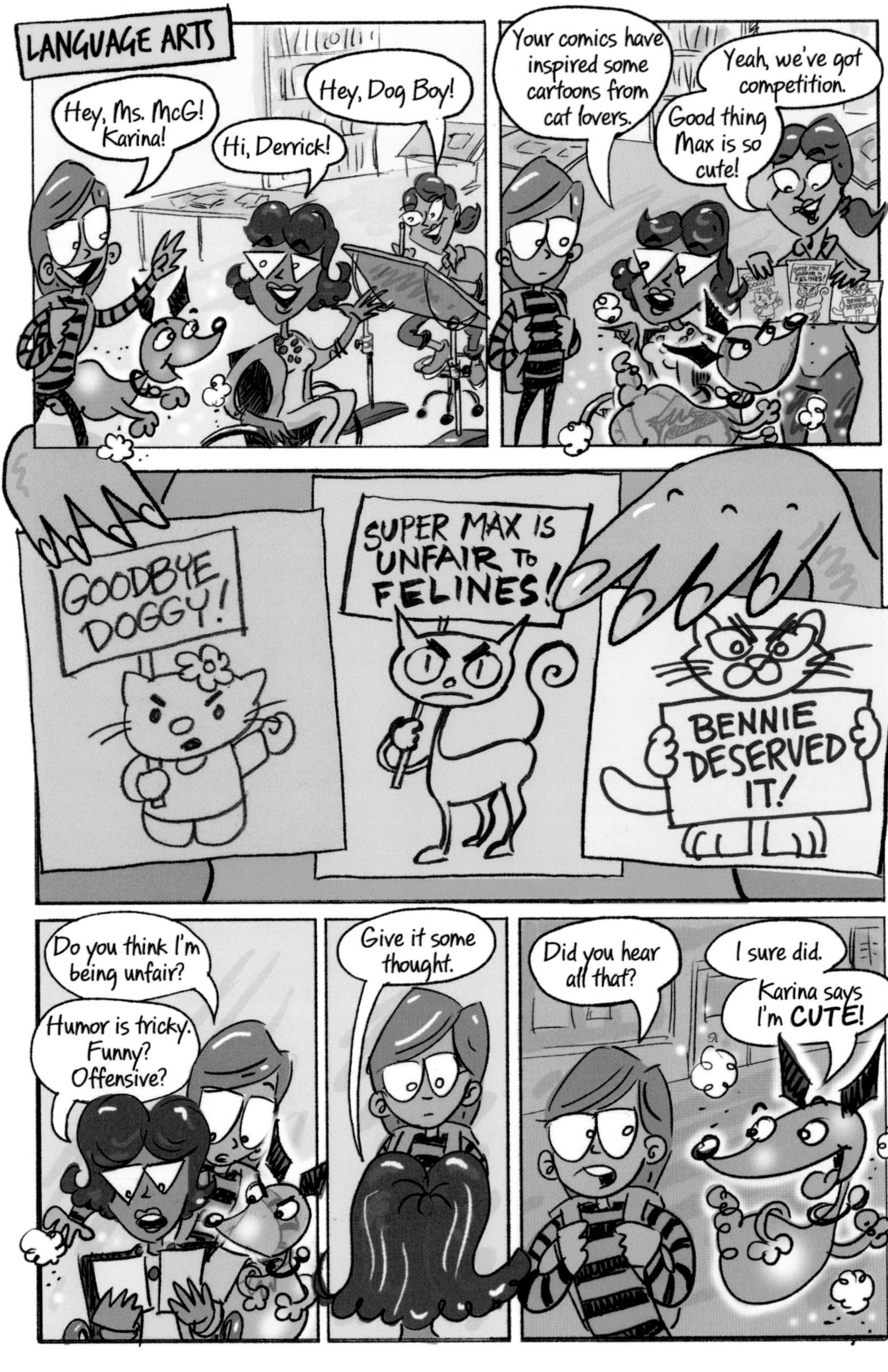

LANGUAGE ARTS
Hey, Ms. McG! Karina!
Hi, Derrick!
Hey, Dog Boy!
Your comics have inspired some cartoons from cat lovers.
Yeah, we've got competition.
Good thing Max is so cute!
GOODBYE DOGGY!
SUPER MAX IS UNFAIR TO FELINES!
BENNIE DESERVED IT!
Do you think I'm being unfair?
Humor is tricky. Funny? Offensive?
Give it some thought.
Did you hear all that?
I sure did.
Karina says I'm CUTE!

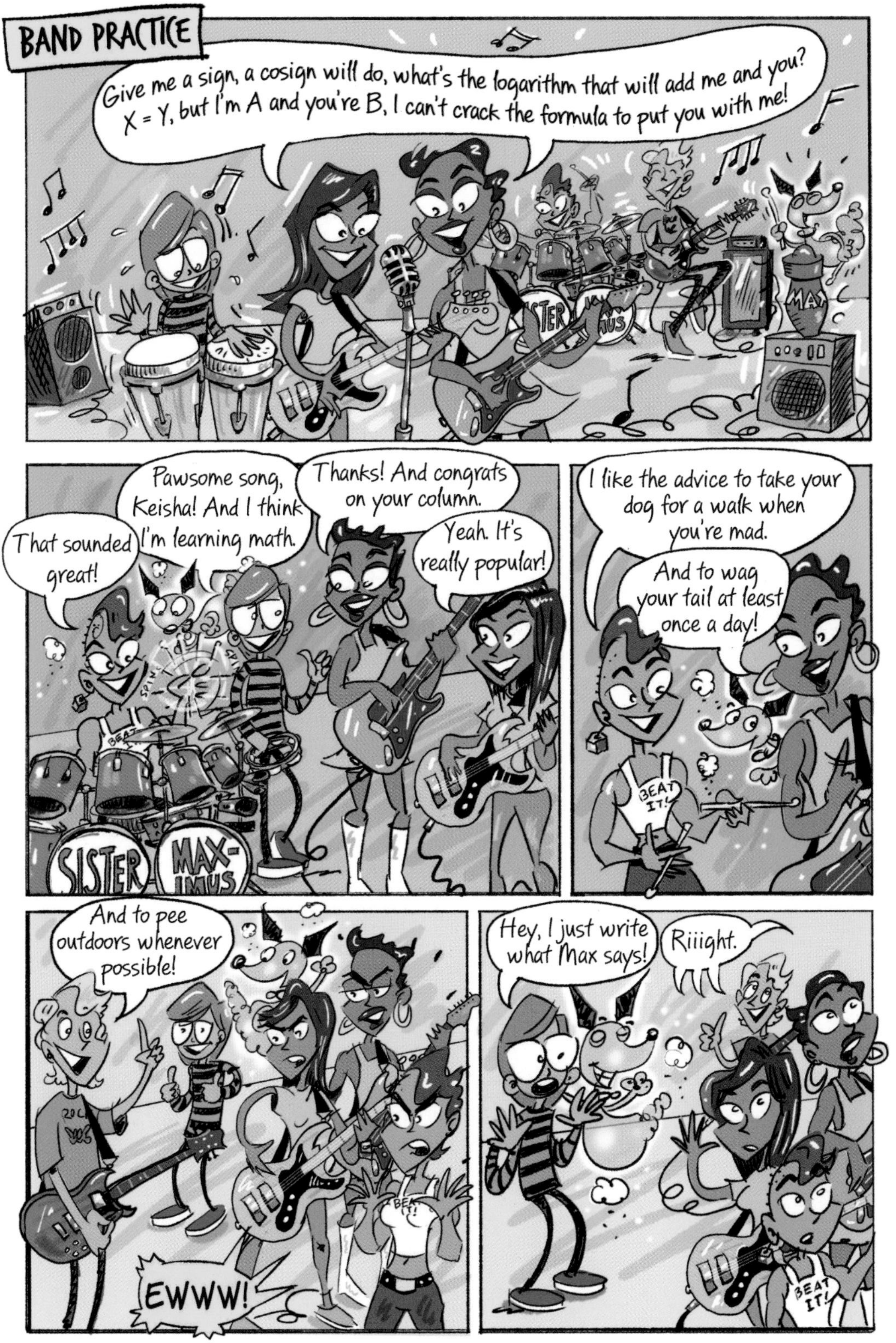
BAND PRACTICE
Give me a sign, a cosign will do, what's the logarithm that will add me and you? X = Y, but I'm A and you're B, I can't crack the formula to put you with me!
MAX
SISTER MAX-IMUS
That sounded great!
Pawsome song, Keisha! And I think I'm learning math.
Thanks! And congrats on your column.
Yeah. It's really popular!
SPIN
BEAT IT!
SISTER
MAX-IMUS
I like the advice to take your dog for a walk when you're mad.
And to wag your tail at least once a day!
BEAT IT!
And to pee outdoors whenever possible!
EWWW!
Hey, I just write what Max says!
Riiight.
BEAT IT!

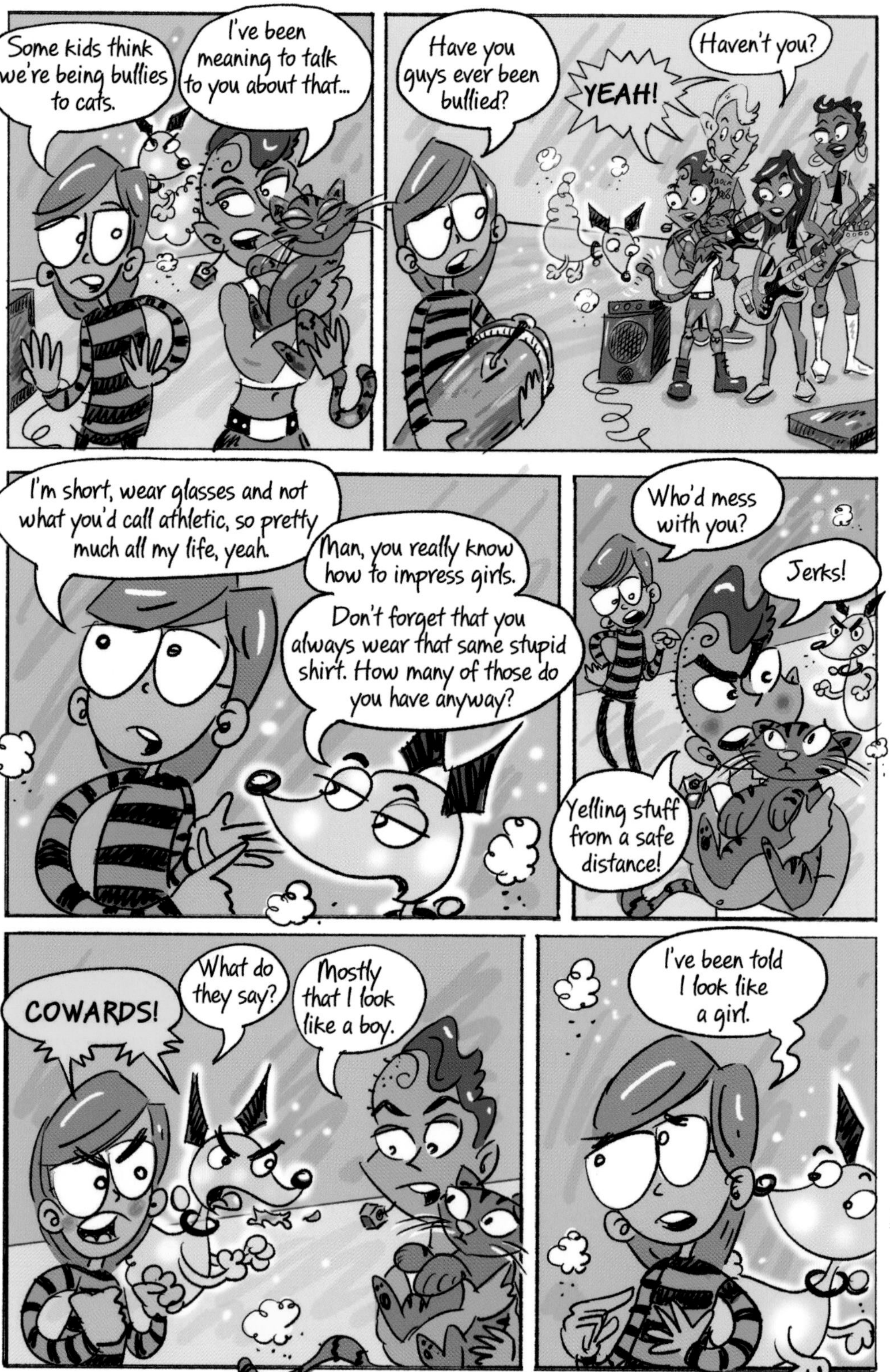

Some kids think we're being bullies to cats.
I've been meaning to talk to you about that...
Have you guys ever been bullied?
YEAH!
Haven't you?
I'm short, wear glasses and not what you'd call athletic, so pretty much all my life, yeah.
Man, you really know how to impress girls.
Don't forget that you always wear that same stupid shirt. How many of those do you have anyway?
Who'd mess with you?
Jerks!
Yelling stuff from a safe distance!
COWARDS!
What do they say?
Mostly that I look like a boy.
I've been told I look like a girl.

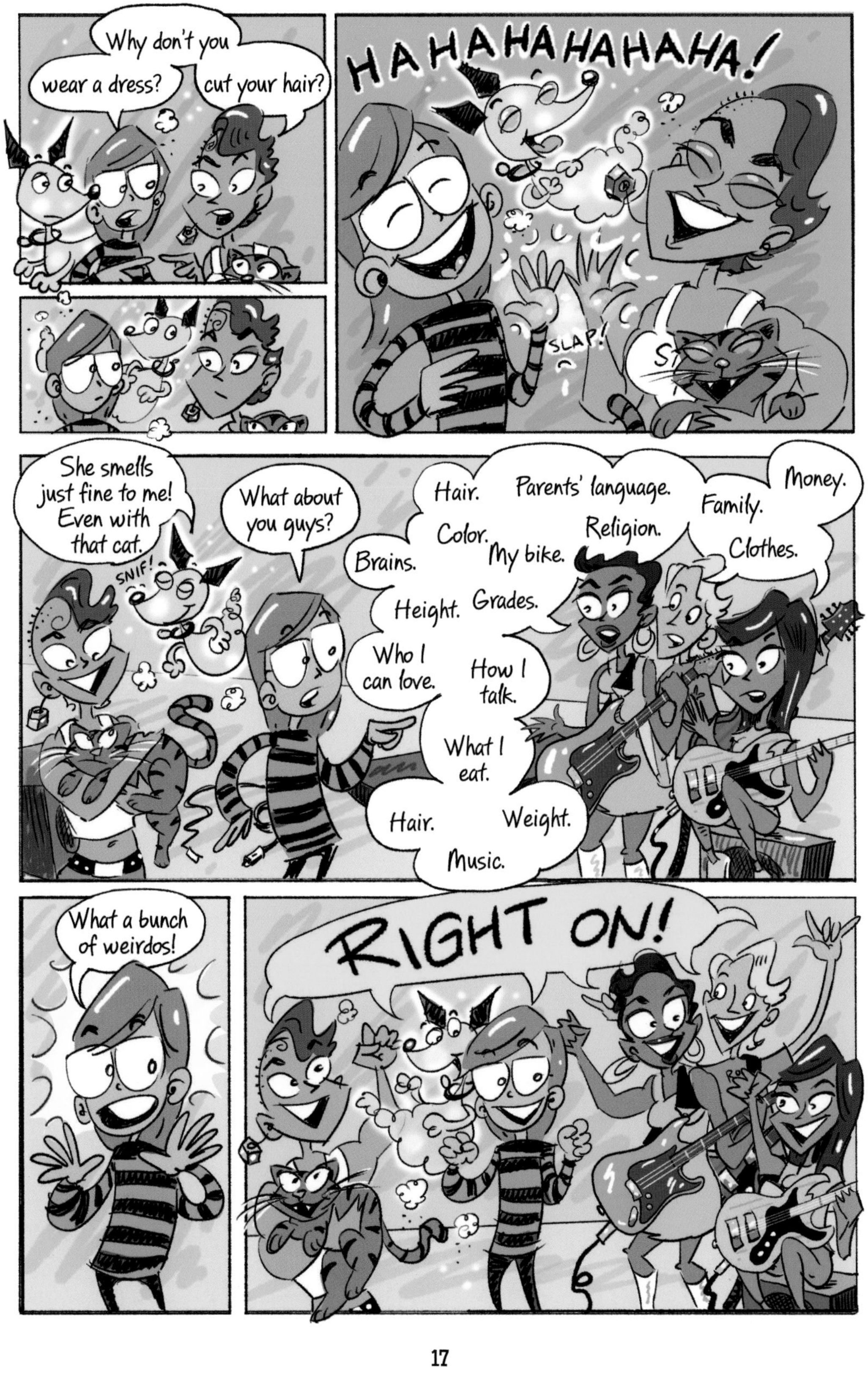
Why don't you
wear a dress?
cut your hair?
HAHAHAHAHAHAHA!
SLAP!
She smells just fine to me! Even with that cat.
SNIF!
What about you guys?
Hair.
Parents' language.
Money.
Family.
Color.
Religion.
Brains.
My bike.
Clothes.
Height.
Grades.
Who I can love.
How I talk.
What I eat.
Hair.
Weight.
Music.
What a bunch of weirdos!
RIGHT ON!

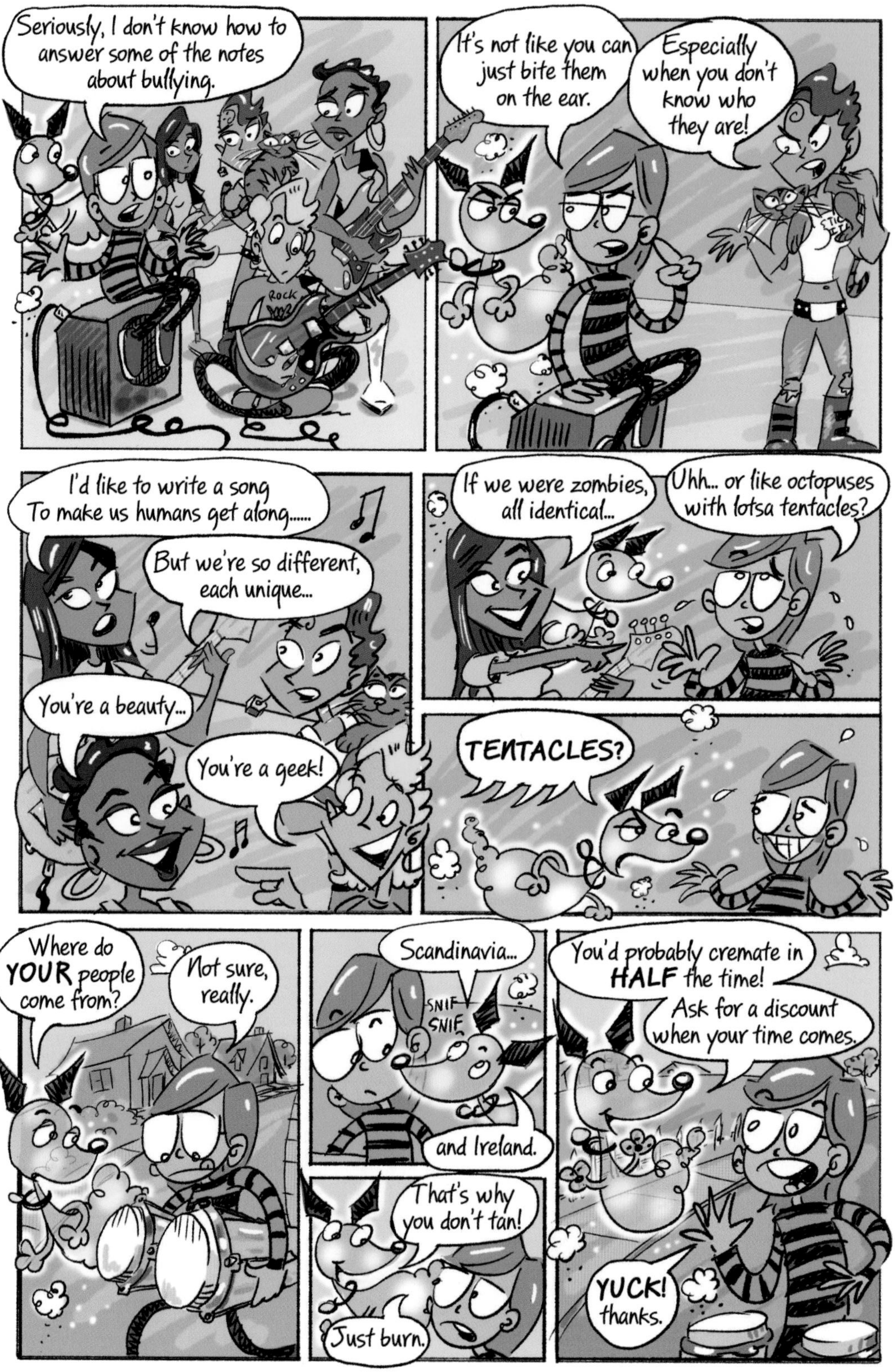

Seriously, I don't know how to answer some of the notes about bullying.
It's not like you can just bite them on the ear.
Especially when you don't know who they are!
I'd like to write a song
To make us humans get along......
But we're so different, each unique...
You're a beauty...
You're a geek!
If we were zombies, all identical...
Uhh... or like octopuses with lotsa tentacles?
TENTACLES?
Where do YOUR people come from?
Not sure, really.
Scandinavia...
SNIF SNIF
and Ireland.
That's why you don't tan!
Just burn.
You'd probably cremate in HALF the time!
Ask for a discount when your time comes.
YUCK! thanks.

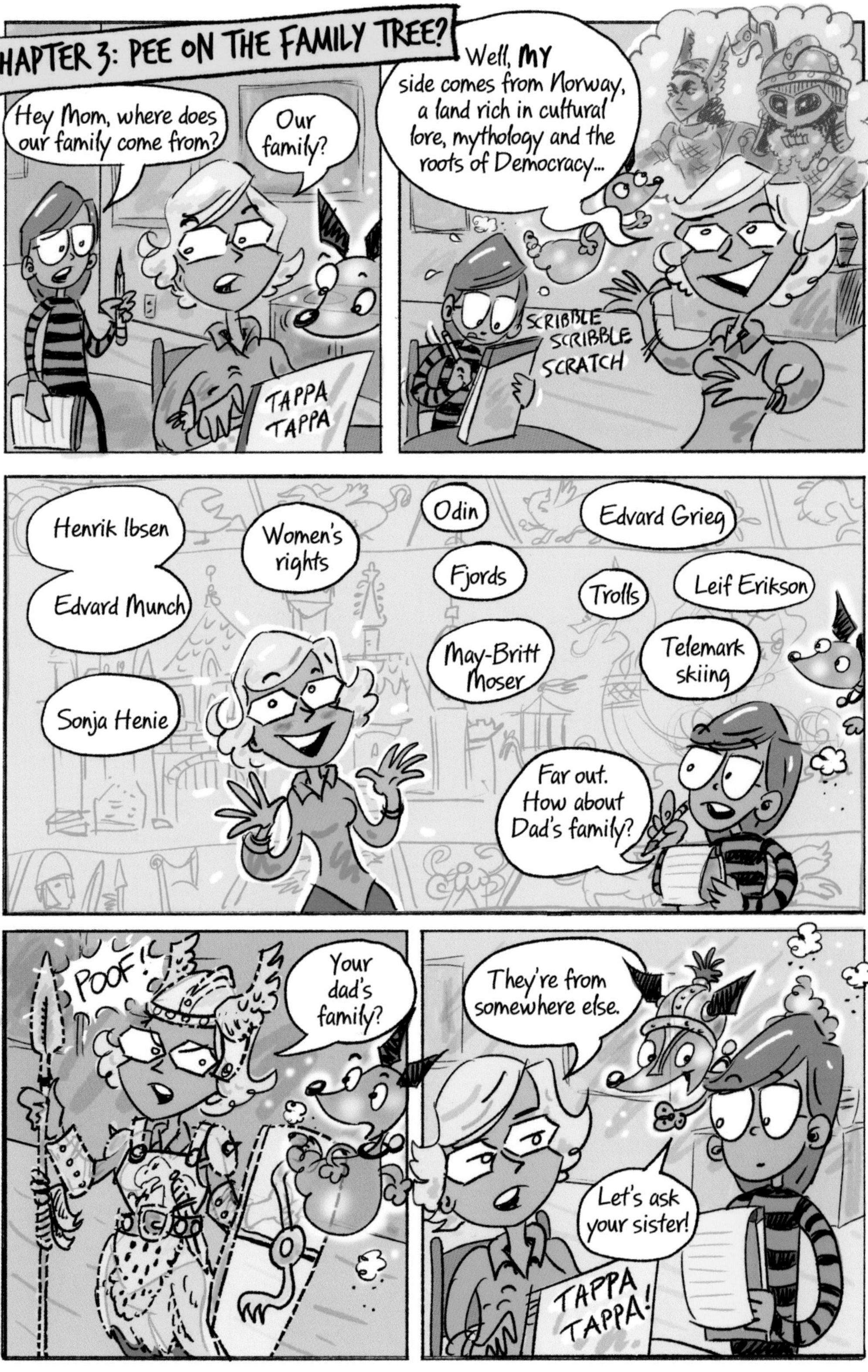

CHAPTER 3: PEE ON THE FAMILY TREE?
Hey Mom, where does our family come from?
Our family?
TAPPA TAPPA
Well, MY side comes from Norway, a land rich in cultural lore, mythology and the roots of Democracy...
SCRIBBLE SCRIBBLE SCRATCH
Henrik Ibsen
Edvard Munch
Women's rights
Odin
Edvard Grieg
Fjords
Trolls
Leif Erikson
May-Britt Moser
Telemark skiing
Sonja Henie
Far out. How about Dad's family?
POOF!
Your dad's family?
They're from somewhere else.
Let's ask your sister!
TAPPA TAPPA!

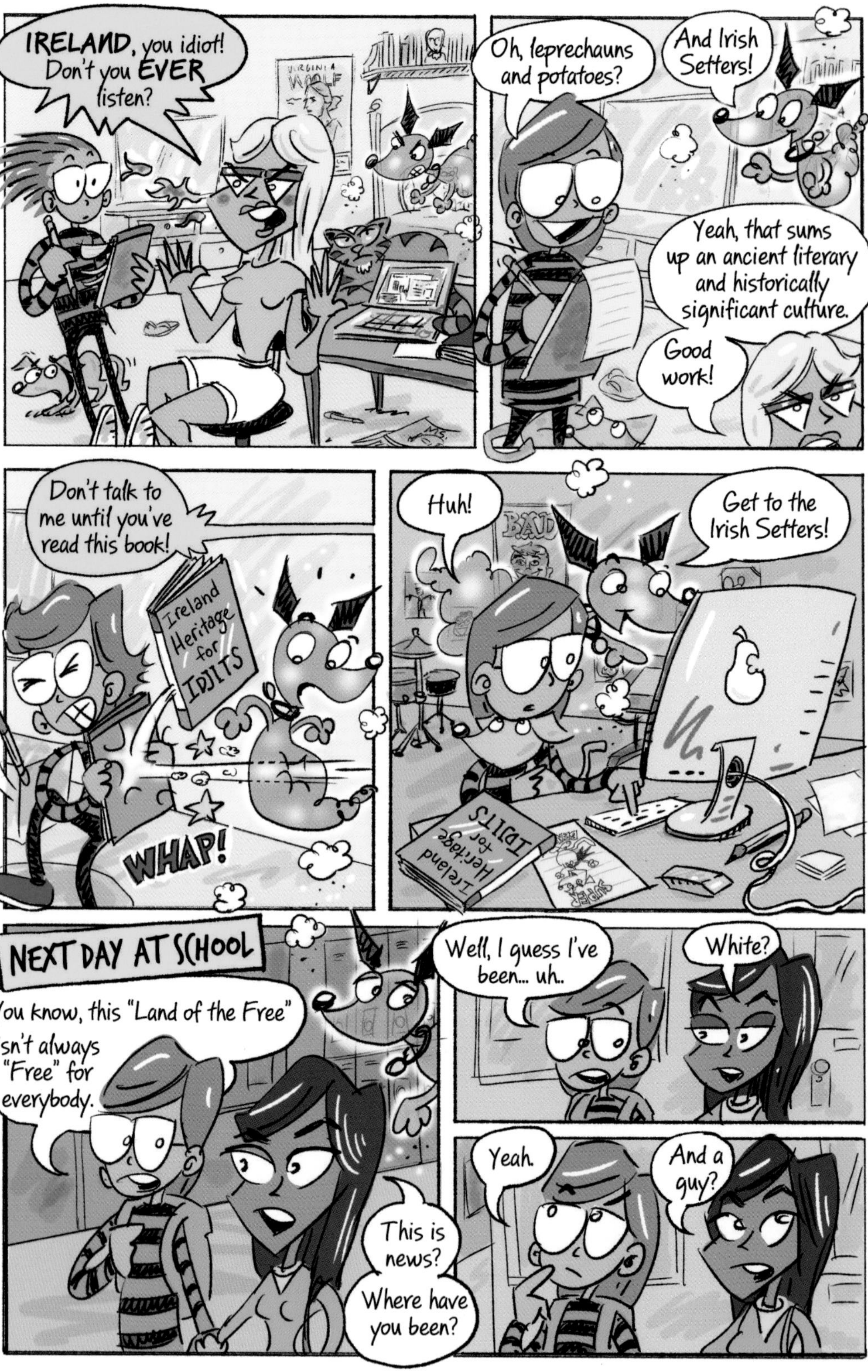

IRELAND, you idiot! Don't you EVER listen?
VIRGINIA WOOLF
Oh, leprechauns and potatoes?
And Irish Setters!
Yeah, that sums up an ancient literary and historically significant culture.
Good work!
Don't talk to me until you've read this book!
Ireland Heritage for IDJITS
WHAP!
Huh!
Get to the Irish Setters!
BAD
Ireland Heritage for IDJITS
NEXT DAY AT SCHOOL
You know, this "Land of the Free" isn't always "Free" for everybody.
This is news?
Where have you been?
Well, I guess I've been... uh..
White?
Yeah.
And a guy?

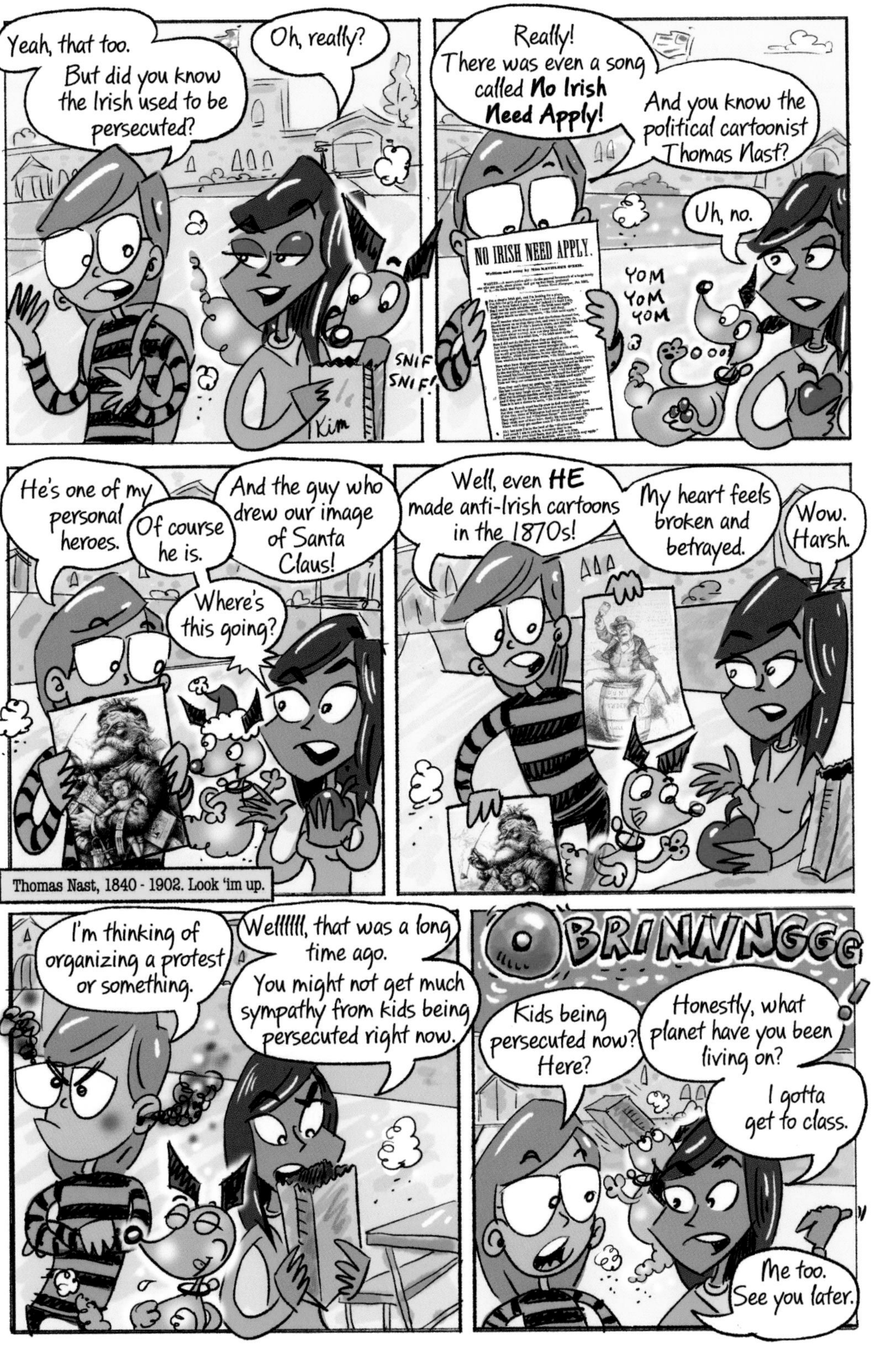

Yeah, that too.
But did you know the Irish used to be persecuted?
Oh, really?
SNIF SNIF!
Kim
Really! There was even a song called **No Irish Need Apply!**
NO IRISH NEED APPLY.
And you know the political cartoonist Thomas Nast?
Uh, no.
YOM YOM YOM
He's one of my personal heroes.
Of course he is.
And the guy who drew our image of Santa Claus!
Where's this going?
Thomas Nast, 1840 - 1902. Look 'im up.
Well, even **HE** made anti-Irish cartoons in the 1870s!
My heart feels broken and betrayed.
Wow. Harsh.
I'm thinking of organizing a protest or something.
Wellllll, that was a long time ago. You might not get much sympathy from kids being persecuted right now.
BRINNNGGG!
Kids being persecuted now? Here?
Honestly, what planet have you been living on?
I gotta get to class.
Me too. See you later.

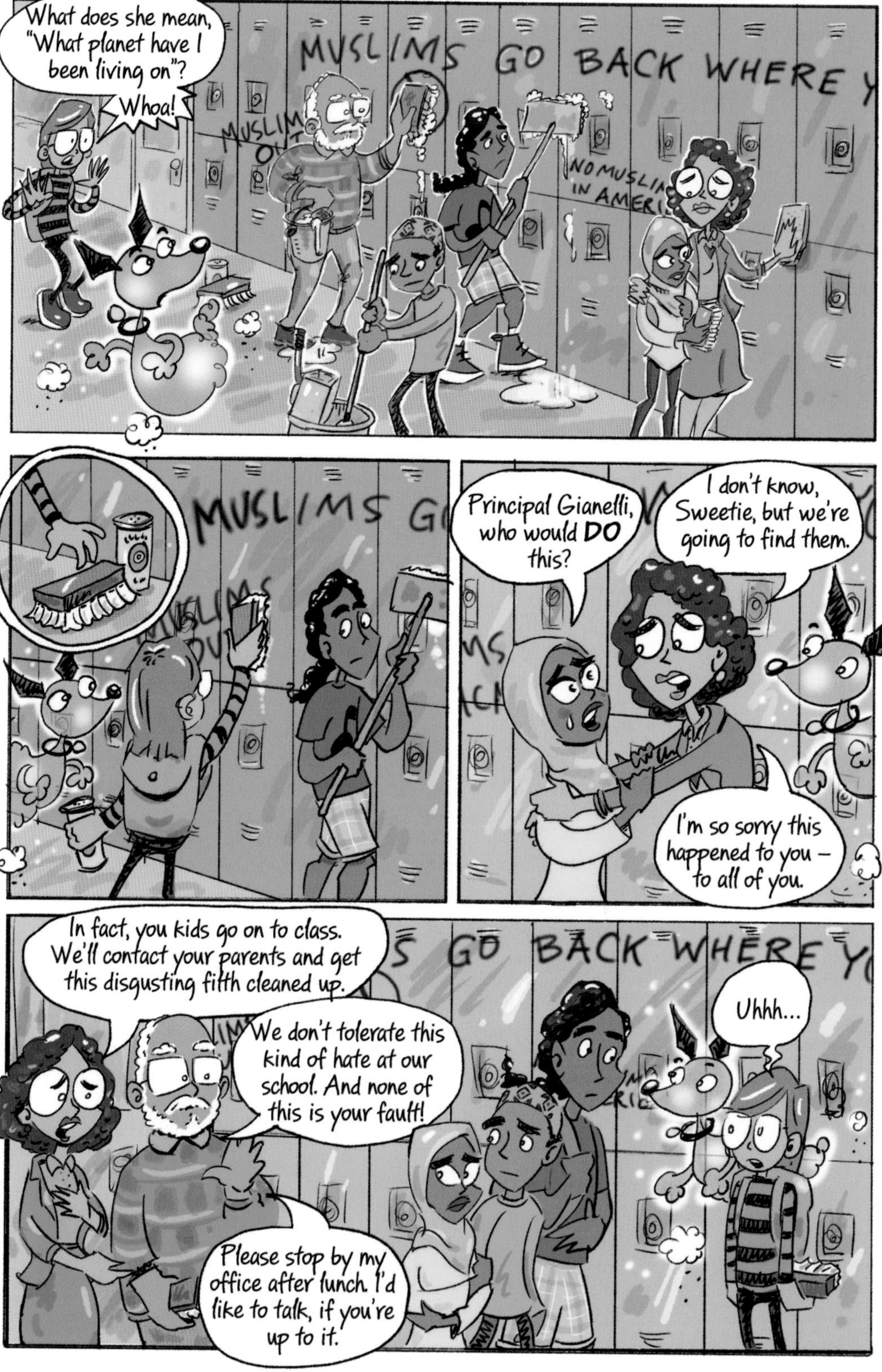

What does she mean, "What planet have I been living on"?
Whoa!
MUSLIMS GO BACK WHERE Y
MUSLIM OUT
NO MUSLIM IN AMERI
MUSLIMS G
Principal Gianelli, who would **DO** this?
I don't know, Sweetie, but we're going to find them.
I'm so sorry this happened to you – to all of you.
In fact, you kids go on to class. We'll contact your parents and get this disgusting filth cleaned up.
S GO BACK WHERE Y
We don't tolerate this kind of hate at our school. And none of this is your fault!
Uhhh...
Please stop by my office after lunch. I'd like to talk, if you're up to it.

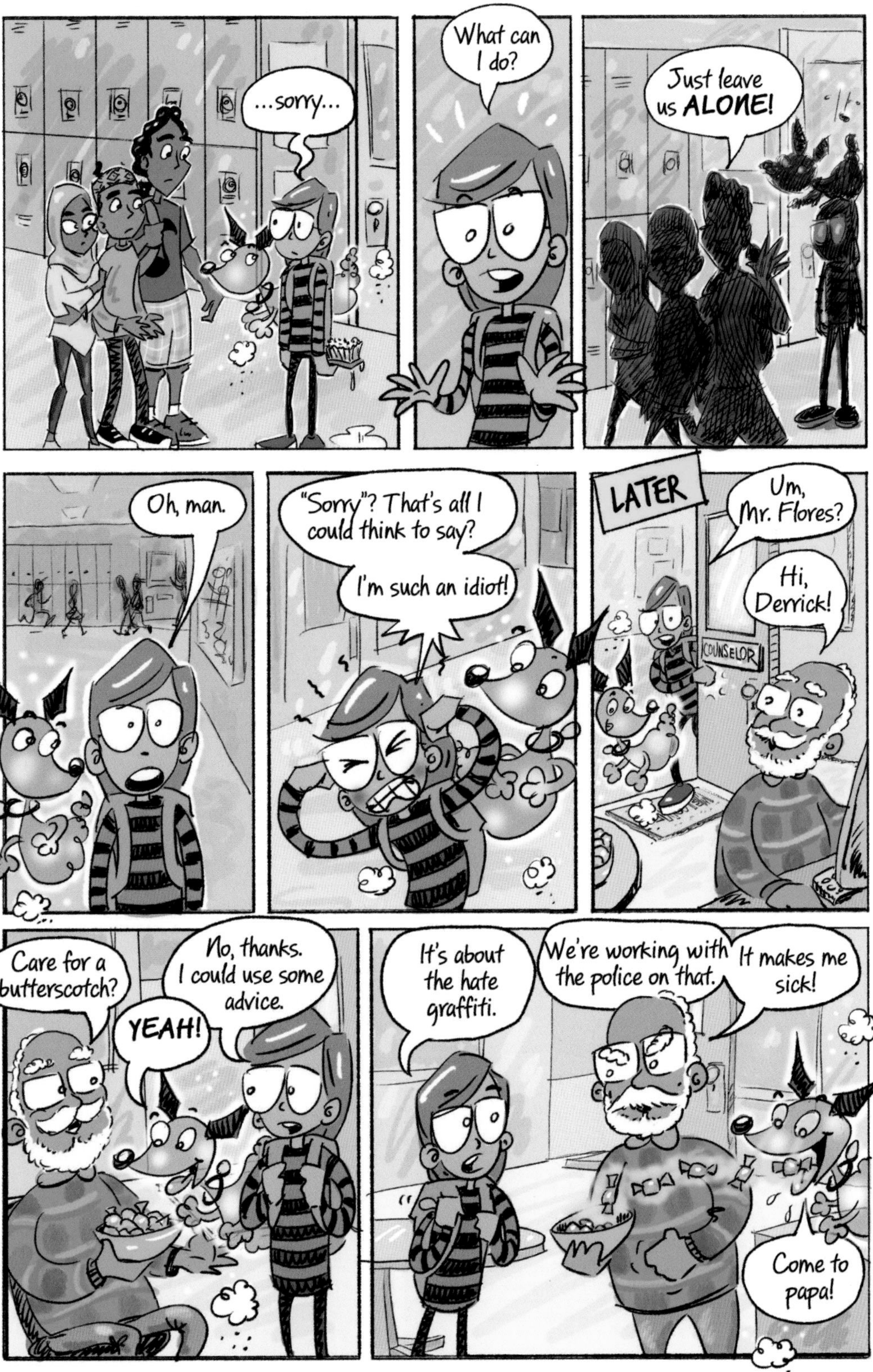
...sorry...
What can I do?
Just leave us ALONE!
Oh, man.
"Sorry"? That's all I could think to say?
I'm such an idiot!
LATER
Um, Mr. Flores?
Hi, Derrick!
COUNSELOR
Care for a butterscotch?
YEAH!
No, thanks. I could use some advice.
It's about the hate graffiti.
We're working with the police on that.
It makes me sick!
Come to papa!

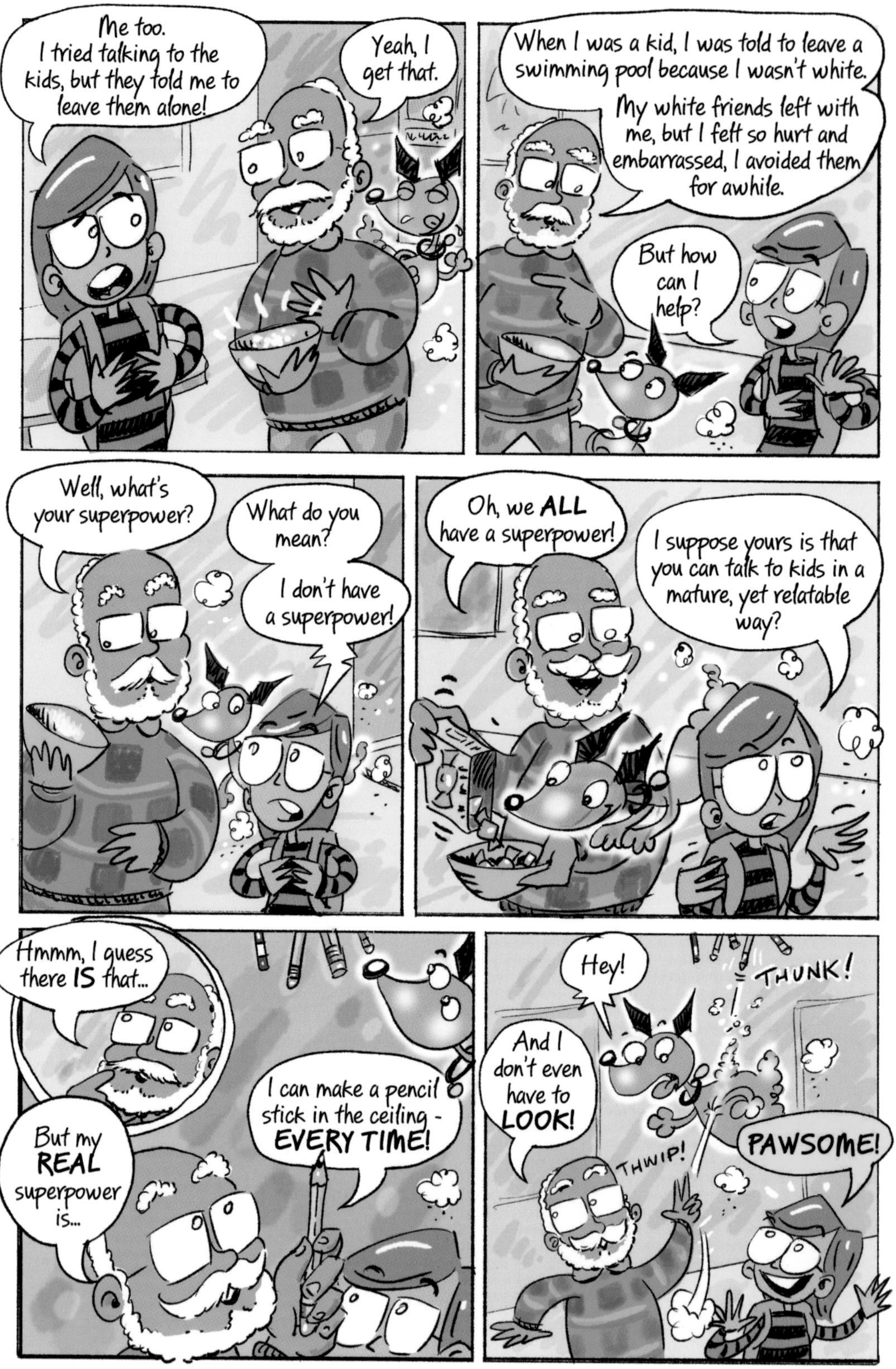
Me too.
I tried talking to the kids, but they told me to leave them alone!
Yeah, I get that.
When I was a kid, I was told to leave a swimming pool because I wasn't white.
My white friends left with me, but I felt so hurt and embarrassed, I avoided them for awhile.
But how can I help?
Well, what's your superpower?
What do you mean?
I don't have a superpower!
Oh, we ALL have a superpower!
I suppose yours is that you can talk to kids in a mature, yet relatable way?
Hmmm, I guess there IS that...
But my REAL superpower is...
I can make a pencil stick in the ceiling - EVERY TIME!
Hey!
THUNK!
And I don't even have to LOOK!
THWIP!
PAWSOME!

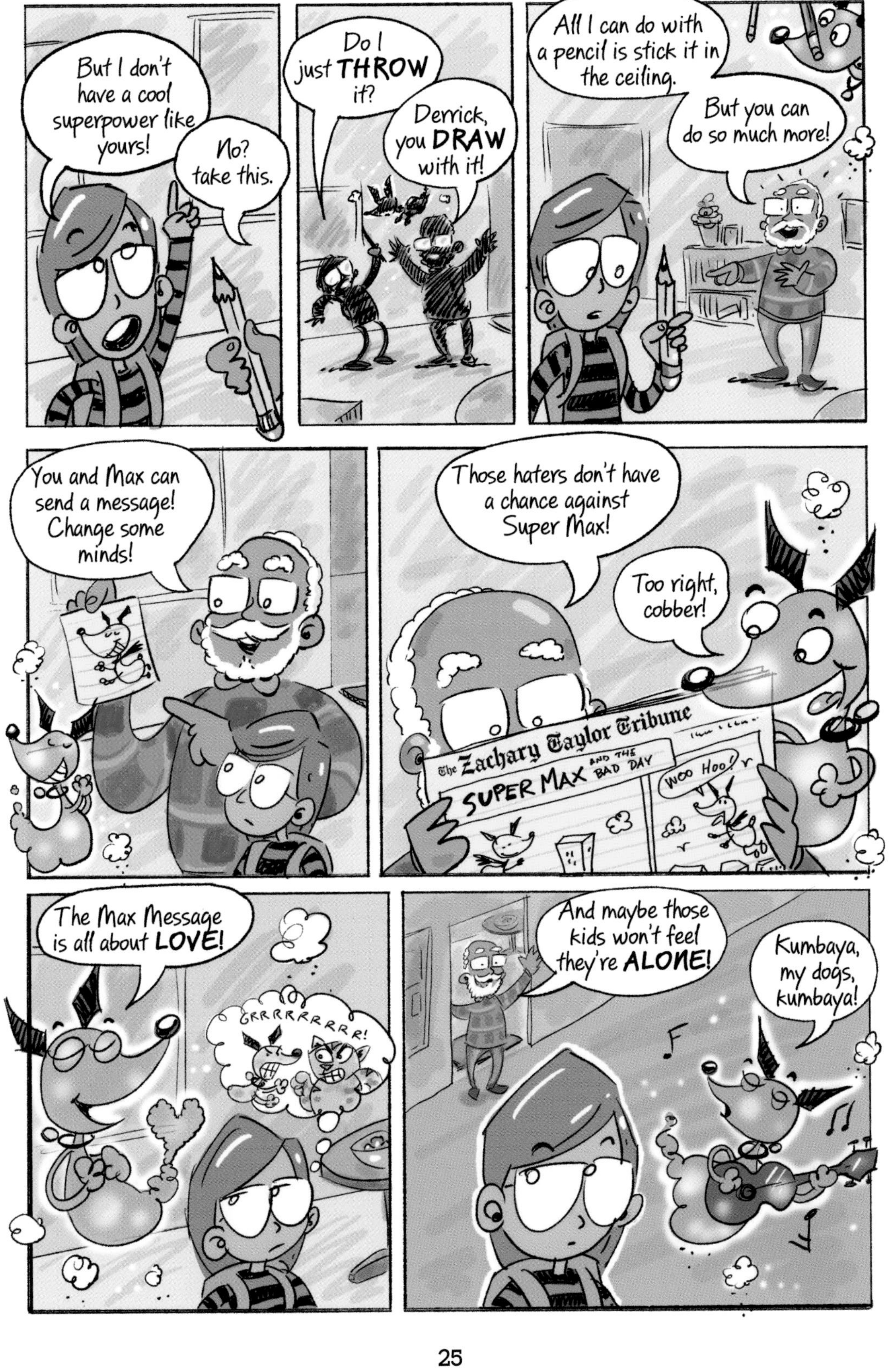

But I don't have a cool superpower like yours!
No? take this.
Do I just **THROW** it?
Derrick, you **DRAW** with it!
All I can do with a pencil is stick it in the ceiling.
But you can do so much more!
You and Max can send a message! Change some minds!
Those haters don't have a chance against Super Max!
Too right, cobber!
The Zachary Taylor Tribune
SUPER MAX AND THE BAD DAY
WOO HOO!
The Max Message is all about **LOVE**!
GRRRRRRRRRR!
And maybe those kids won't feel they're **ALONE**!
Kumbaya, my dogs, kumbaya!

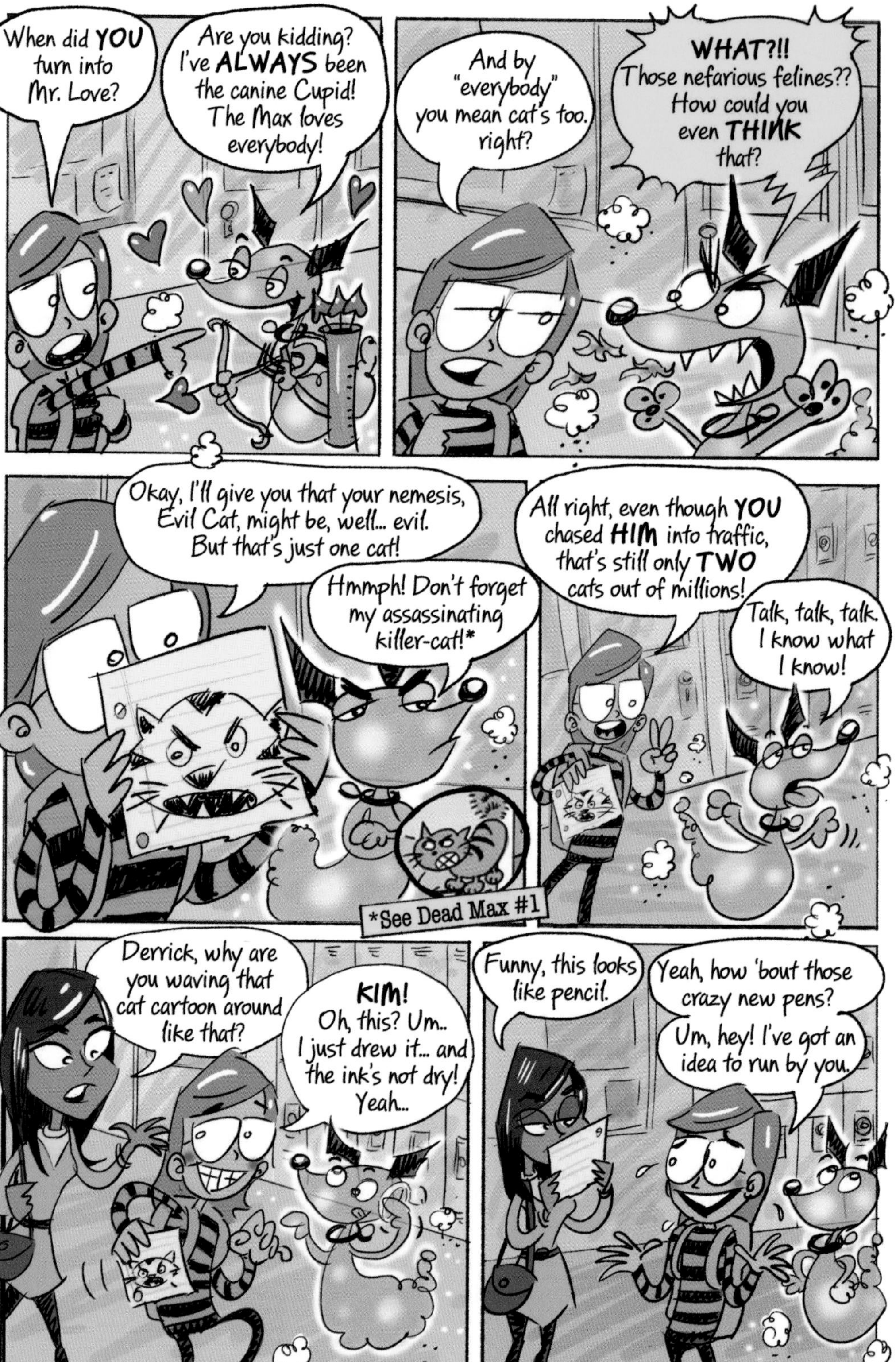

When did YOU turn into Mr. Love?
Are you kidding? I've ALWAYS been the canine Cupid! The Max loves everybody!
And by "everybody" you mean cat's too. right?
WHAT?!! Those nefarious felines?? How could you even THINK that?
Okay, I'll give you that your nemesis, Evil Cat, might be, well... evil. But that's just one cat!
Hmmph! Don't forget my assassinating killer-cat!*
*See Dead Max #1
All right, even though YOU chased HIM into traffic, that's still only TWO cats out of millions!
Talk, talk, talk. I know what I know!
Derrick, why are you waving that cat cartoon around like that?
KIM! Oh, this? Um.. I just drew it... and the ink's not dry! Yeah...
Funny, this looks like pencil.
Yeah, how 'bout those crazy new pens?
Um, hey! I've got an idea to run by you.

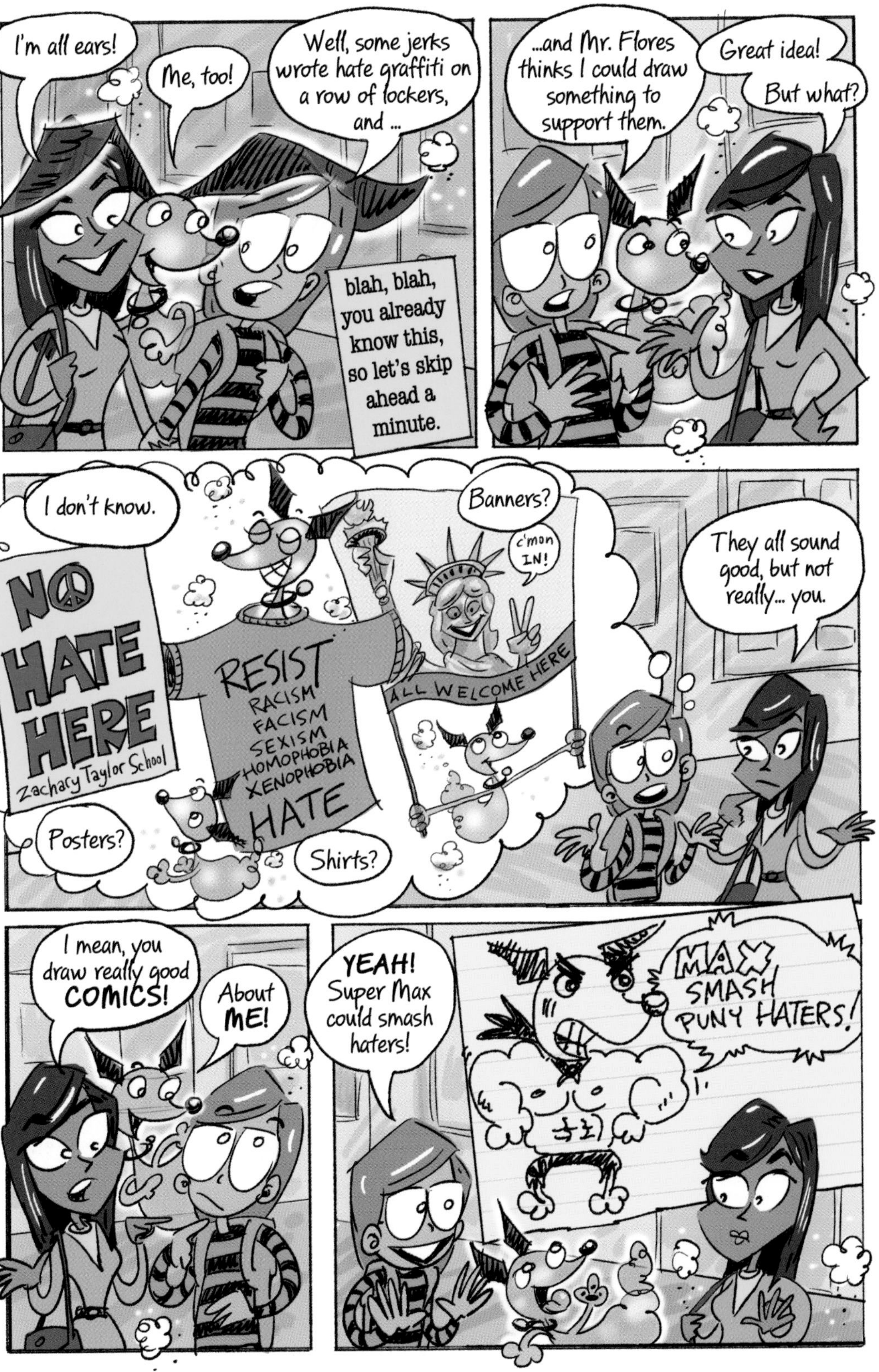

I'm all ears!
Me, too!
Well, some jerks wrote hate graffiti on a row of lockers, and ...
blah, blah, you already know this, so let's skip ahead a minute.
...and Mr. Flores thinks I could draw something to support them.
Great idea!
But what?
I don't know.
NO HATE HERE
Zachary Taylor School
RESIST RACISM FACISM SEXISM HOMOPHOBIA XENOPHOBIA HATE
Banners?
c'mon IN!
ALL WELCOME HERE
Posters?
Shirts?
They all sound good, but not really... you.
I mean, you draw really good COMICS!
About ME!
YEAH! Super Max could smash haters!
MAX SMASH PUNY HATERS!

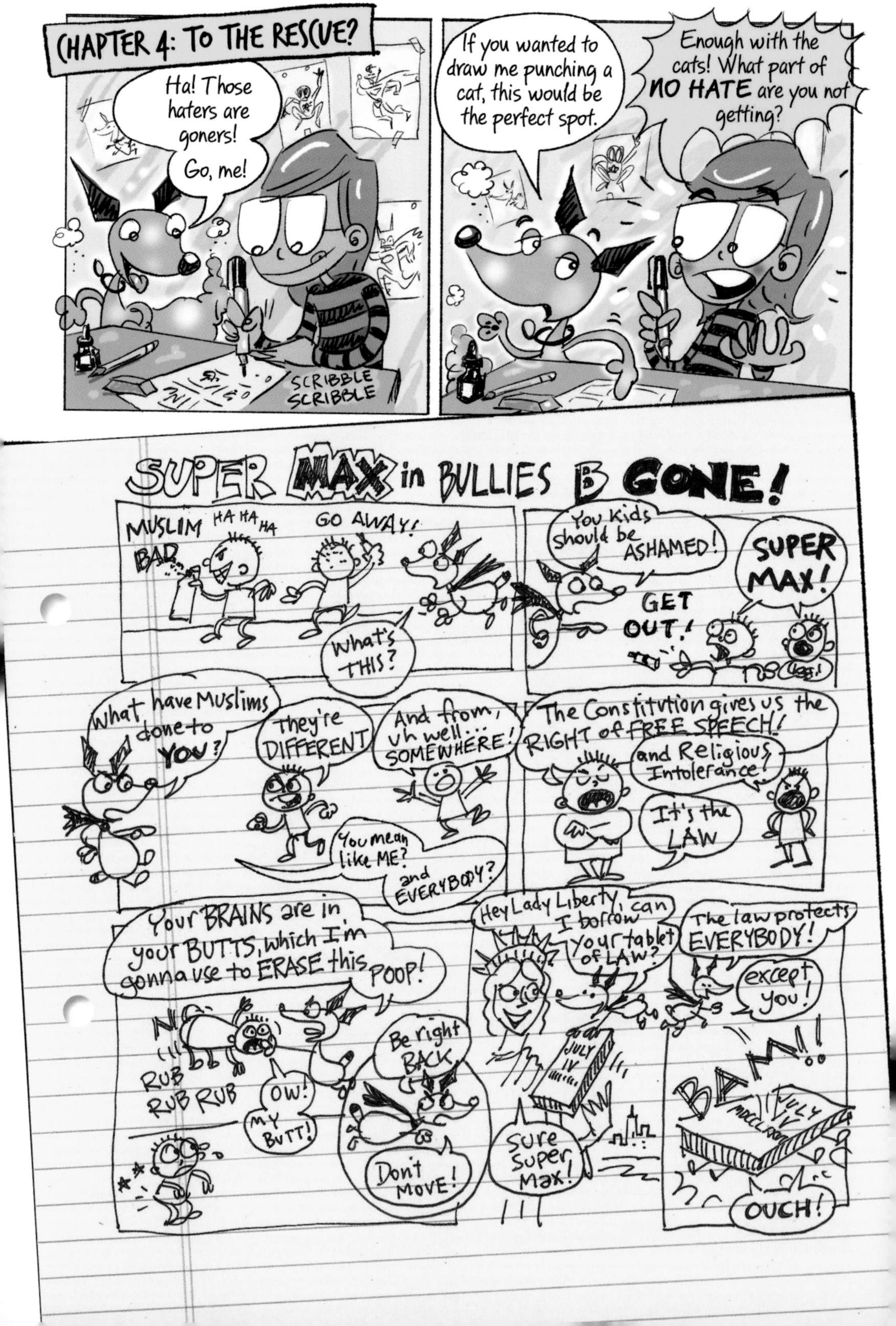
CHAPTER 4: TO THE RESCUE?
Ha! Those haters are goners!
Go, me!
SCRIBBLE SCRIBBLE
If you wanted to draw me punching a cat, this would be the perfect spot.
Enough with the cats! What part of NO HATE are you not getting?
SUPER MAX in BULLIES B GONE!
MUSLIM BAD
HA HA HA
GO AWAY!
What's THIS?
You Kids should be ASHAMED!
GET OUT!
SUPER MAX!
What have Muslims done to YOU?
They're DIFFERENT
And from, uh well... SOMEWHERE!
You mean like ME? and EVERYBODY?
The Constitution gives us the RIGHT of FREE SPEECH!
and Religious Intolerance!
It's the LAW
Your BRAINS are in your BUTTS, which I'm gonna use to ERASE this POOP!
RUB RUB RUB
OW! MY BUTT!
Be right BACK
Don't MOVE!
Hey Lady Liberty, can I borrow your tablet of LAW?
JULY IV
Sure Super Max!
The law protects EVERYBODY!
except you!
BAM!!
OUCH!

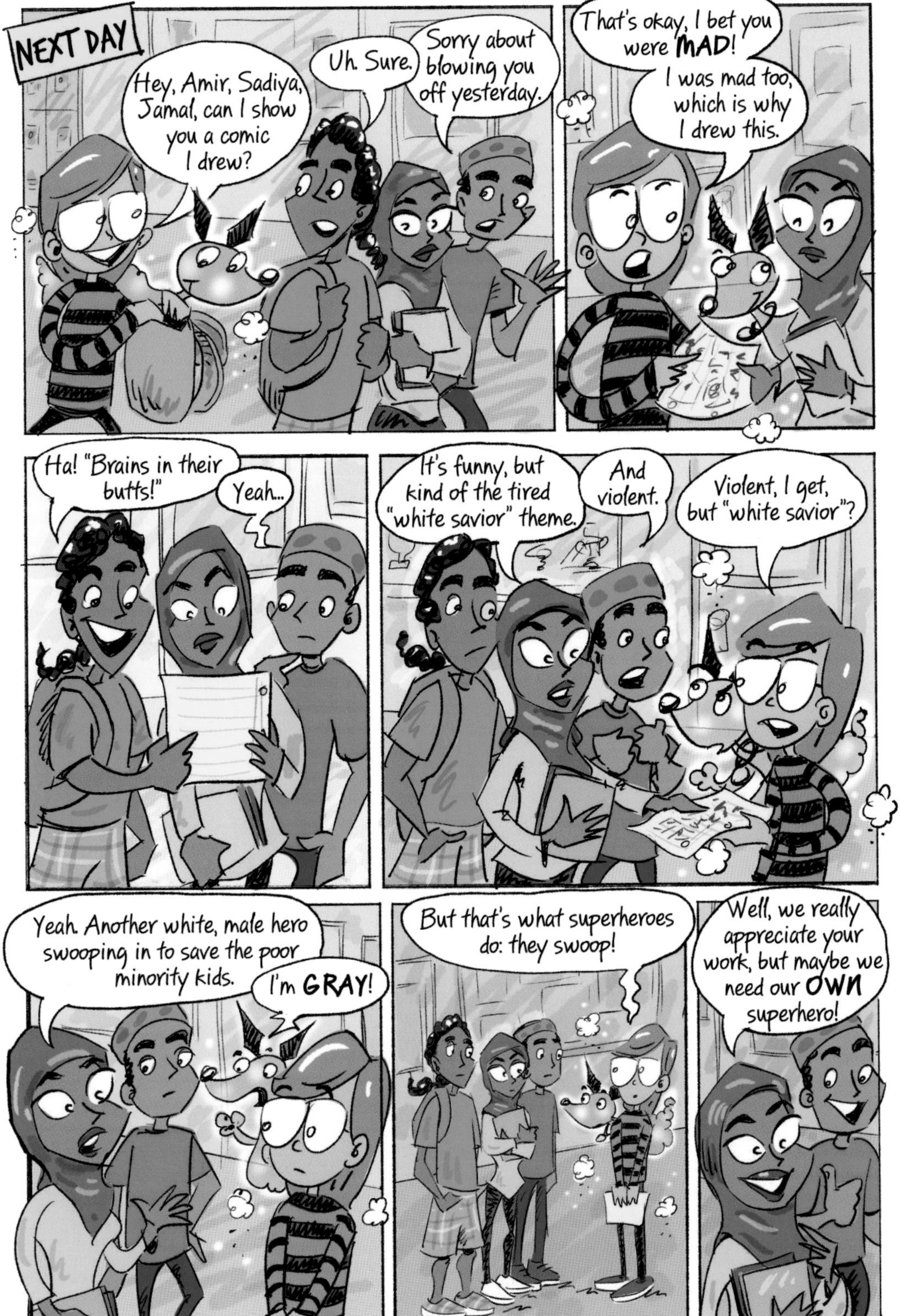
NEXT DAY
Hey, Amir, Sadiya, Jamal, can I show you a comic I drew?
Uh. Sure.
Sorry about blowing you off yesterday.
That's okay, I bet you were MAD!
I was mad too, which is why I drew this.
Ha! "Brains in their butts!"
Yeah...
It's funny, but kind of the tired "white savior" theme.
And violent.
Violent, I get, but "white savior"?
Yeah. Another white, male hero swooping in to save the poor minority kids.
I'm GRAY!
But that's what superheroes do: they swoop!
Well, we really appreciate your work, but maybe we need our OWN superhero!

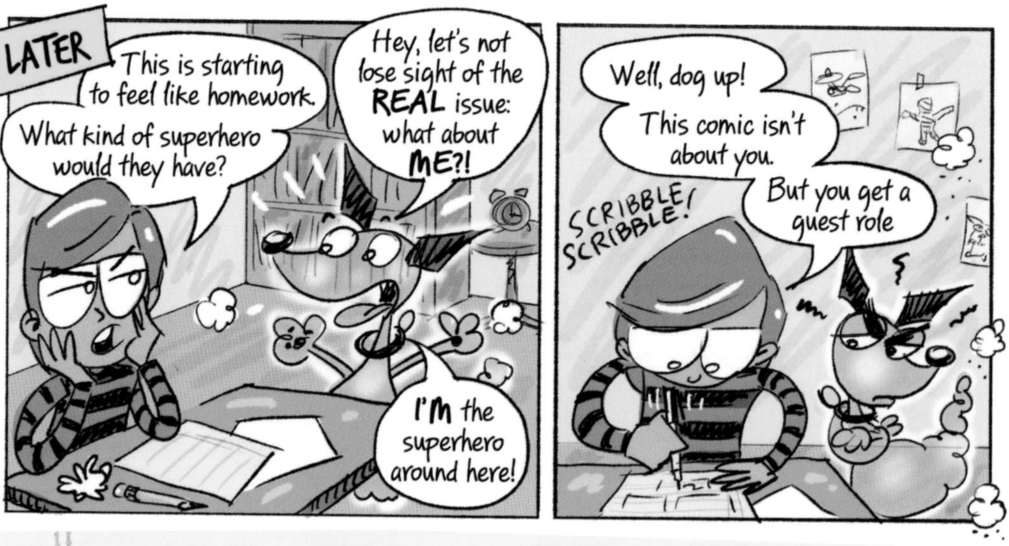
LATER
This is starting to feel like homework.
What kind of superhero would they have?
Hey, let's not lose sight of the REAL issue: what about ME?!
I'M the superhero around here!
Well, dog up!
This comic isn't about you.
But you get a guest role
SCRIBBLE SCRIBBLE!

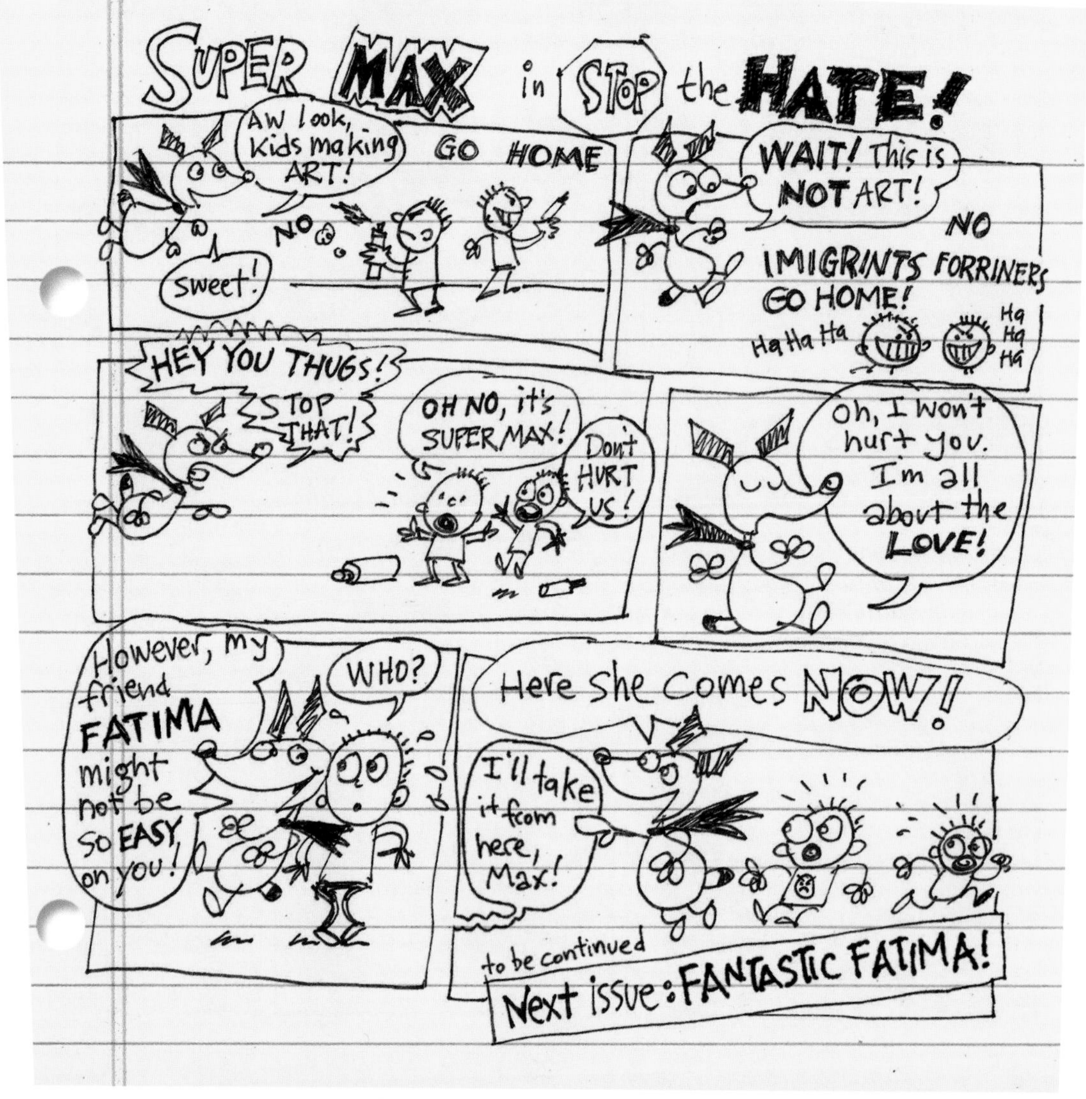
SUPER MAX in STOP the HATE!
Aw look, kids making ART!
sweet!
NO
GO HOME
WAIT! This is NOT ART!
NO IMIGRINTS FORRINERS GO HOME!
Ha Ha Ha
Ha Ha Ha
HEY YOU THUGS!
STOP THAT!
OH NO, it's SUPER MAX!
Don't HURT US!
Oh, I won't hurt you. I'm all about the LOVE!
However, my friend FATIMA might not be so EASY on you!
WHO?
Here she comes NOW!
I'll take it from here, Max!
to be continued
Next issue: FANTASTIC FATIMA!

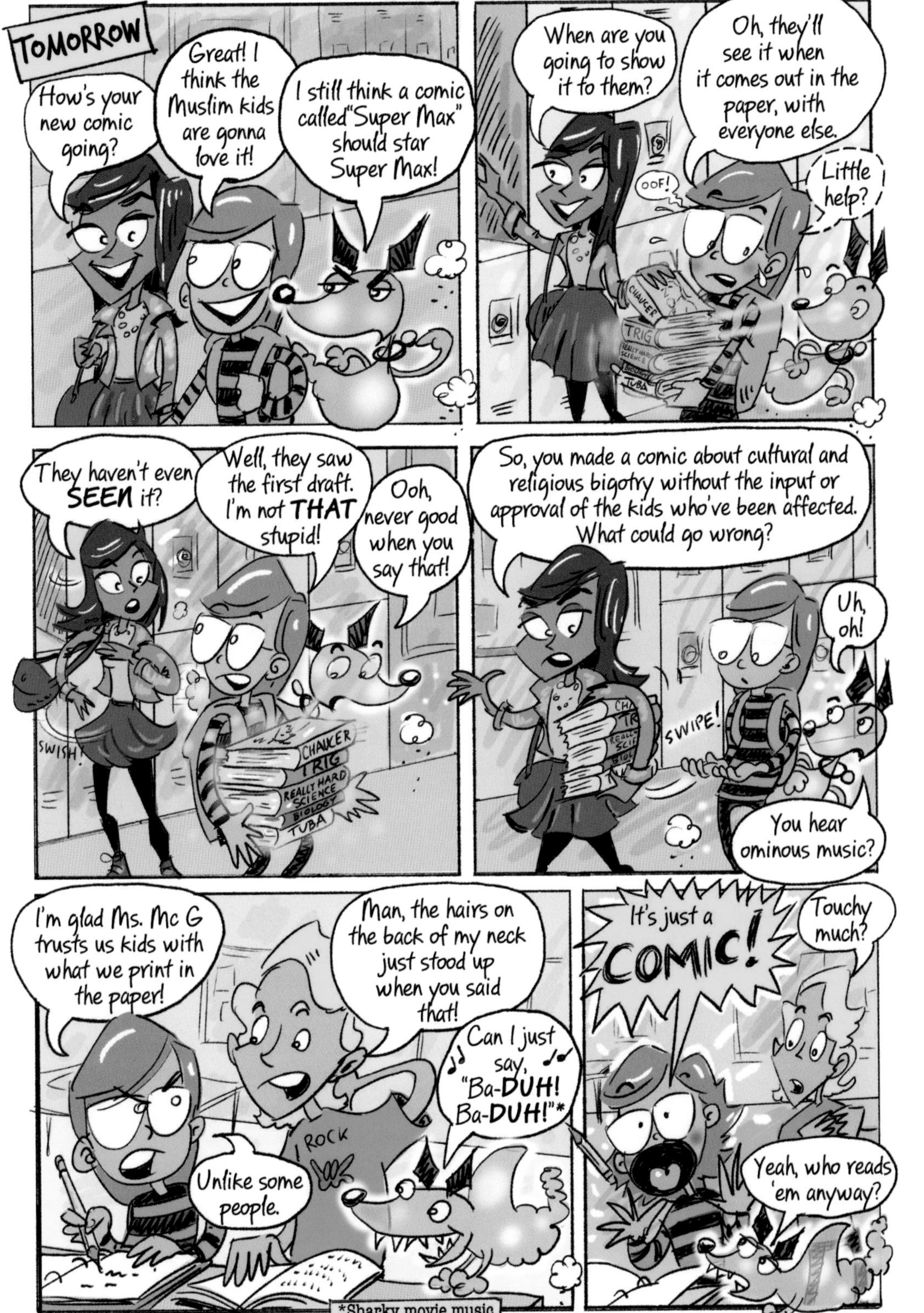
TOMORROW
How's your new comic going?
Great! I think the Muslim kids are gonna love it!
I still think a comic called "Super Max" should star Super Max!
When are you going to show it to them?
Oh, they'll see it when it comes out in the paper, with everyone else.
OOF!
Little help?
CHAUCER
TRIG
REALLY HARD SCIENCE
BIOLOGY
TUBA
They haven't even SEEN it?
Well, they saw the first draft. I'm not THAT stupid!
Ooh, never good when you say that!
SWISH!
So, you made a comic about cultural and religious bigotry without the input or approval of the kids who've been affected. What could go wrong?
Uh, oh!
SWIPE!
You hear ominous music?
I'm glad Ms. Mc G trusts us kids with what we print in the paper!
Man, the hairs on the back of my neck just stood up when you said that!
Can I just say, "Ba-DUH! Ba-DUH!"*
ROCK
Unlike some people.
It's just a COMIC!
Touchy much?
Yeah, who reads 'em anyway?
*Sharky movie music

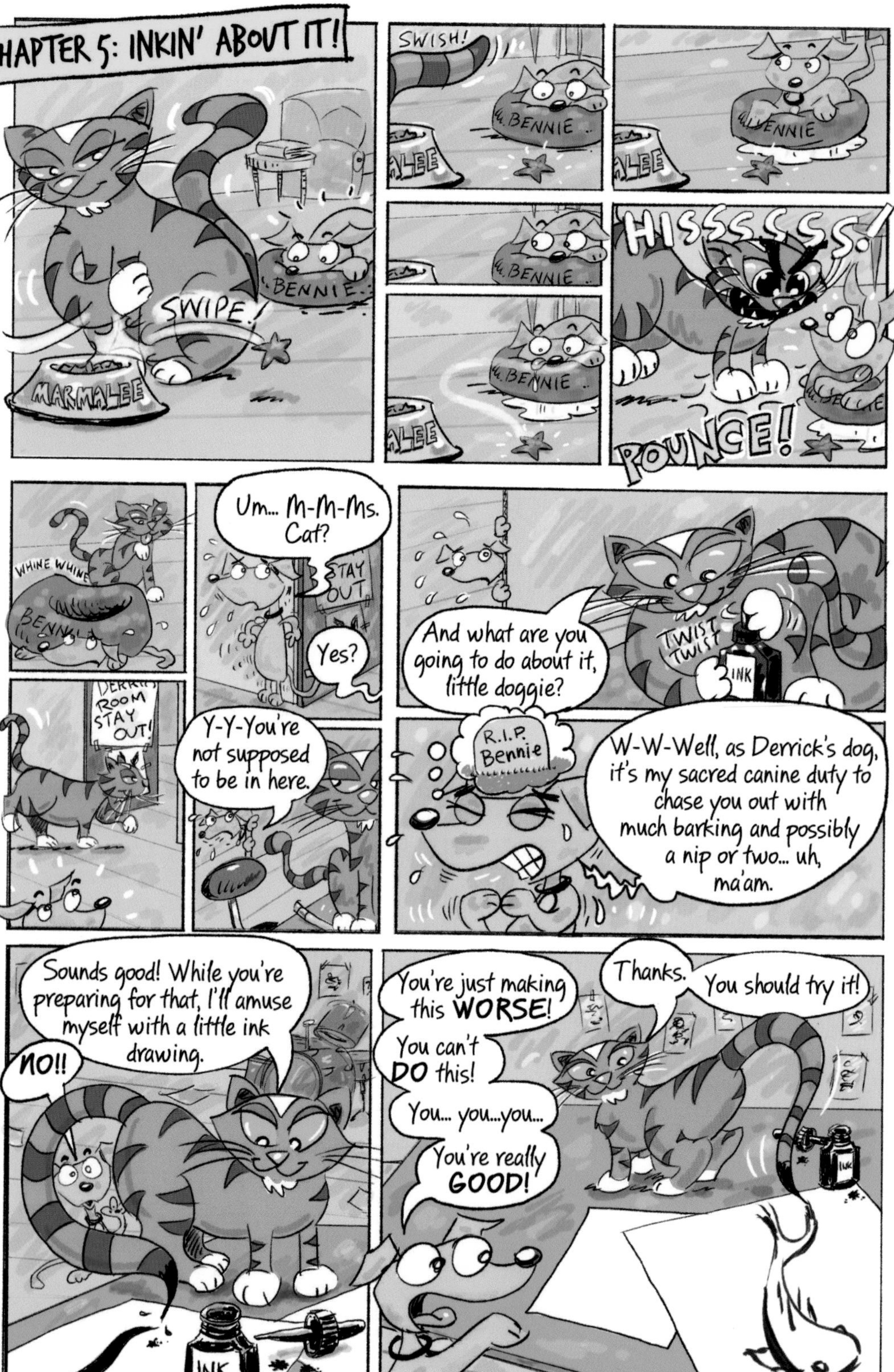
CHAPTER 5: INKIN' ABOUT IT!
MARMALEE
BENNIE
SWIPE!
SWISH!
BENNIE
BENNIE
BENNIE
BENNIE
HISSSSSS!
POUNCE!
WHINE WHINE
Um... M-M-Ms. Cat?
STAY OUT
Yes?
And what are you going to do about it, little doggie?
TWIST TWIST
INK
ROOM STAY OUT!
Y-Y-You're not supposed to be in here.
R.I.P. Bennie
W-W-Well, as Derrick's dog, it's my sacred canine duty to chase you out with much barking and possibly a nip or two... uh, ma'am.
Sounds good! While you're preparing for that, I'll amuse myself with a little ink drawing.
NO!!
INK
You're just making this WORSE!
You can't DO this!
You... you...you...
You're really GOOD!
Thanks.
You should try it!
INK

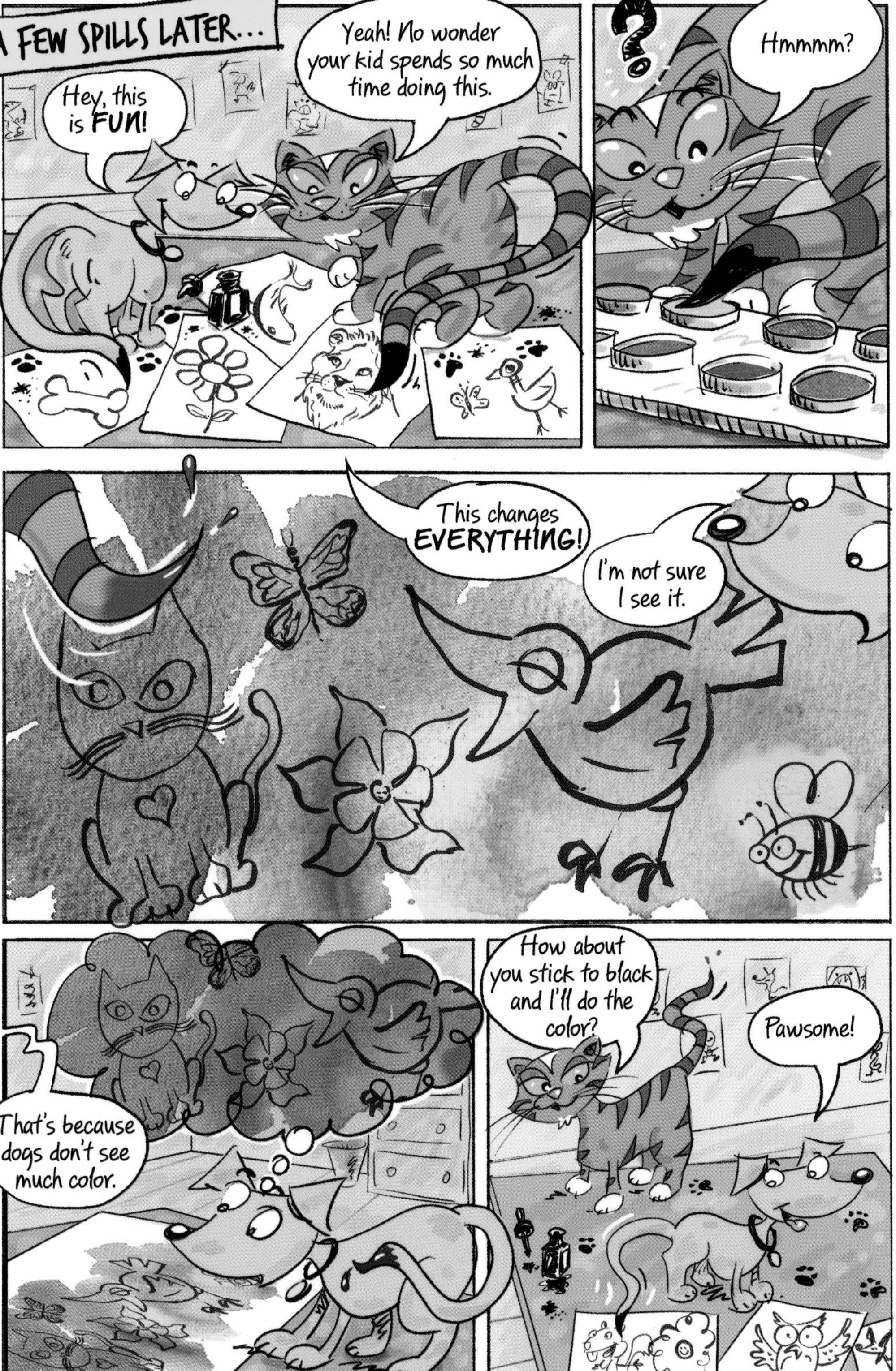
A FEW SPILLS LATER...
Hey, this is FUN!
Yeah! No wonder your kid spends so much time doing this.
Hmmmm?
This changes EVERYTHING!
I'm not sure I see it.
That's because dogs don't see much color.
How about you stick to black and I'll do the color?
Pawsome!

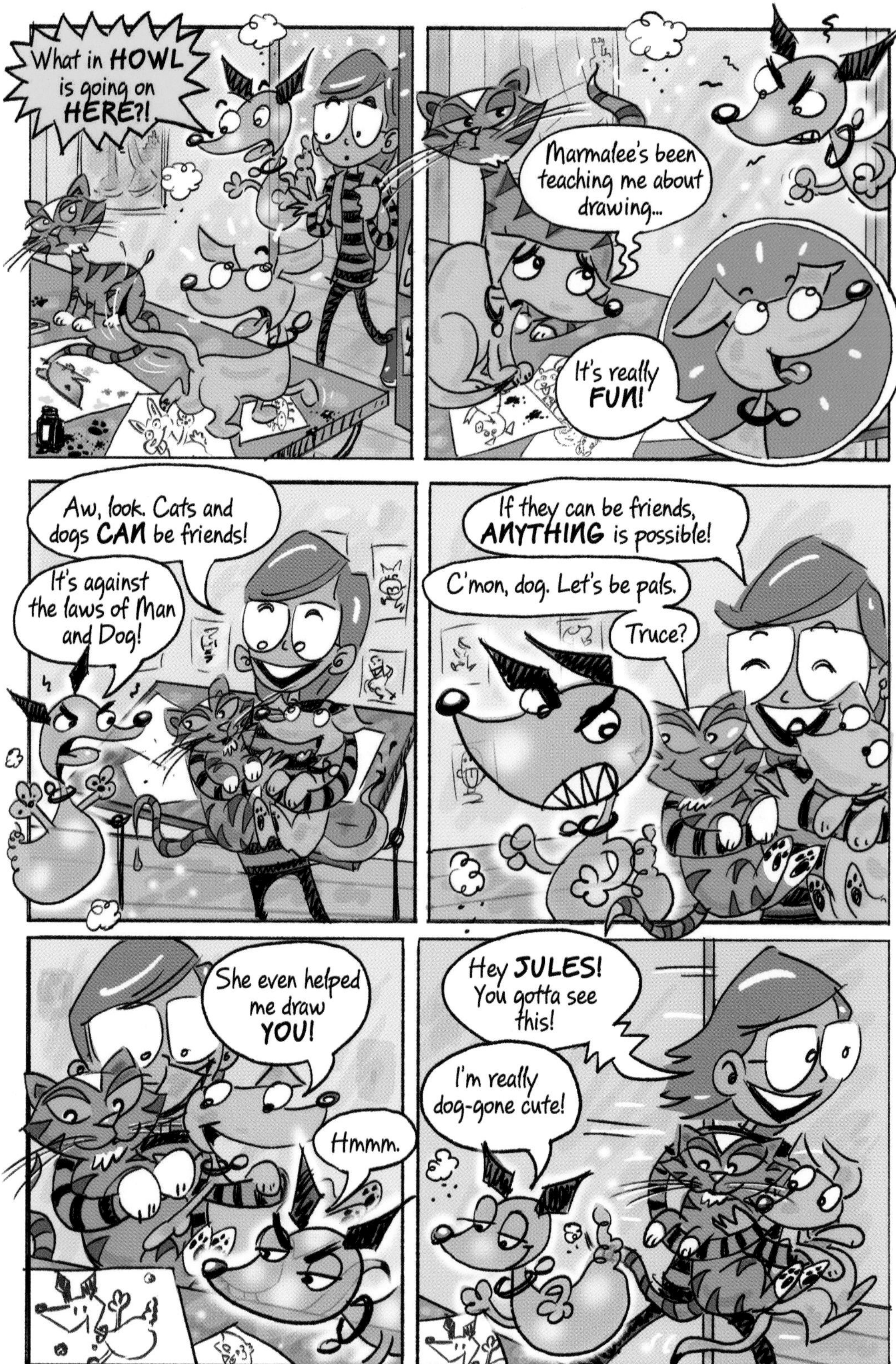
What in HOWL is going on HERE?!
Marmalee's been teaching me about drawing...
It's really FUN!
Aw, look. Cats and dogs CAN be friends!
It's against the laws of Man and Dog!
If they can be friends, ANYTHING is possible!
C'mon, dog. Let's be pals.
Truce?
She even helped me draw YOU!
Hmmm.
Hey JULES! You gotta see this!
I'm really dog-gone cute!

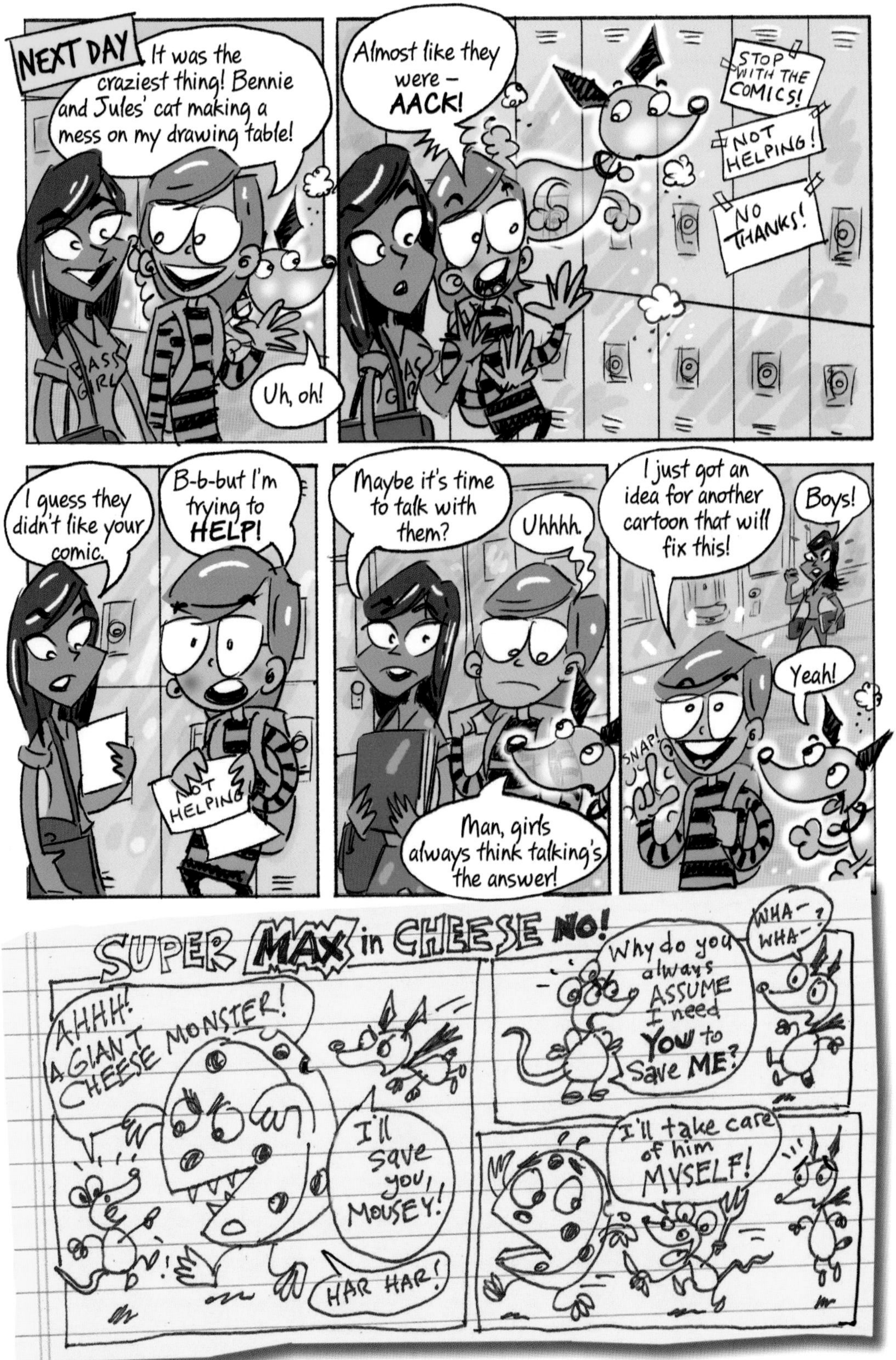
NEXT DAY
It was the craziest thing! Bennie and Jules' cat making a mess on my drawing table!
Uh, oh!
Almost like they were – AACK!
STOP WITH THE COMICS!
NOT HELPING!
NO THANKS!
I guess they didn't like your comic.
B-b-but I'm trying to HELP!
NOT HELPING
Maybe it's time to talk with them?
Uhhhh.
Man, girls always think talking's the answer!
I just got an idea for another cartoon that will fix this!
SNAP!
Boys!
Yeah!
SUPER MAX in CHEESE NO!
AHHH! A GIANT CHEESE MONSTER!
I'll save you, MOUSEY!
HAR HAR!
Why do you always ASSUME I need YOU to Save ME?
WHA- WHA-?
I'll take care of him MYSELF!

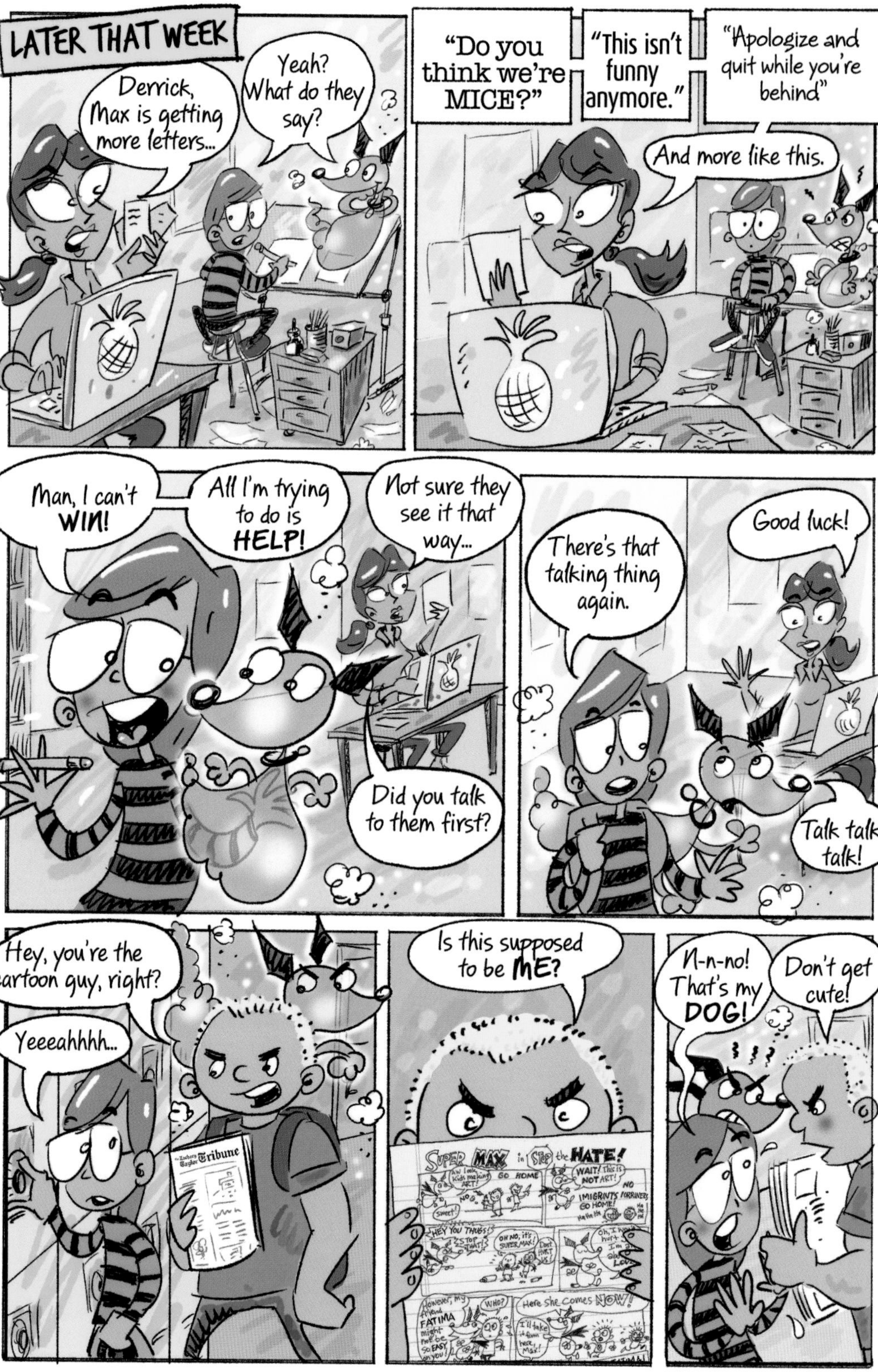
LATER THAT WEEK
Derrick, Max is getting more letters...
Yeah? What do they say?
"Do you think we're MICE?"
"This isn't funny anymore."
"Apologize and quit while you're behind"
And more like this.
Man, I can't WIN!
All I'm trying to do is HELP!
Not sure they see it that way...
Did you talk to them first?
There's that talking thing again.
Good luck!
Talk talk, talk!
Hey, you're the cartoon guy, right?
Yeeeahhhh...
Is this supposed to be ME?
SUPER MAX in STOP the HATE!
N-n-no! That's my DOG!
Don't get cute!

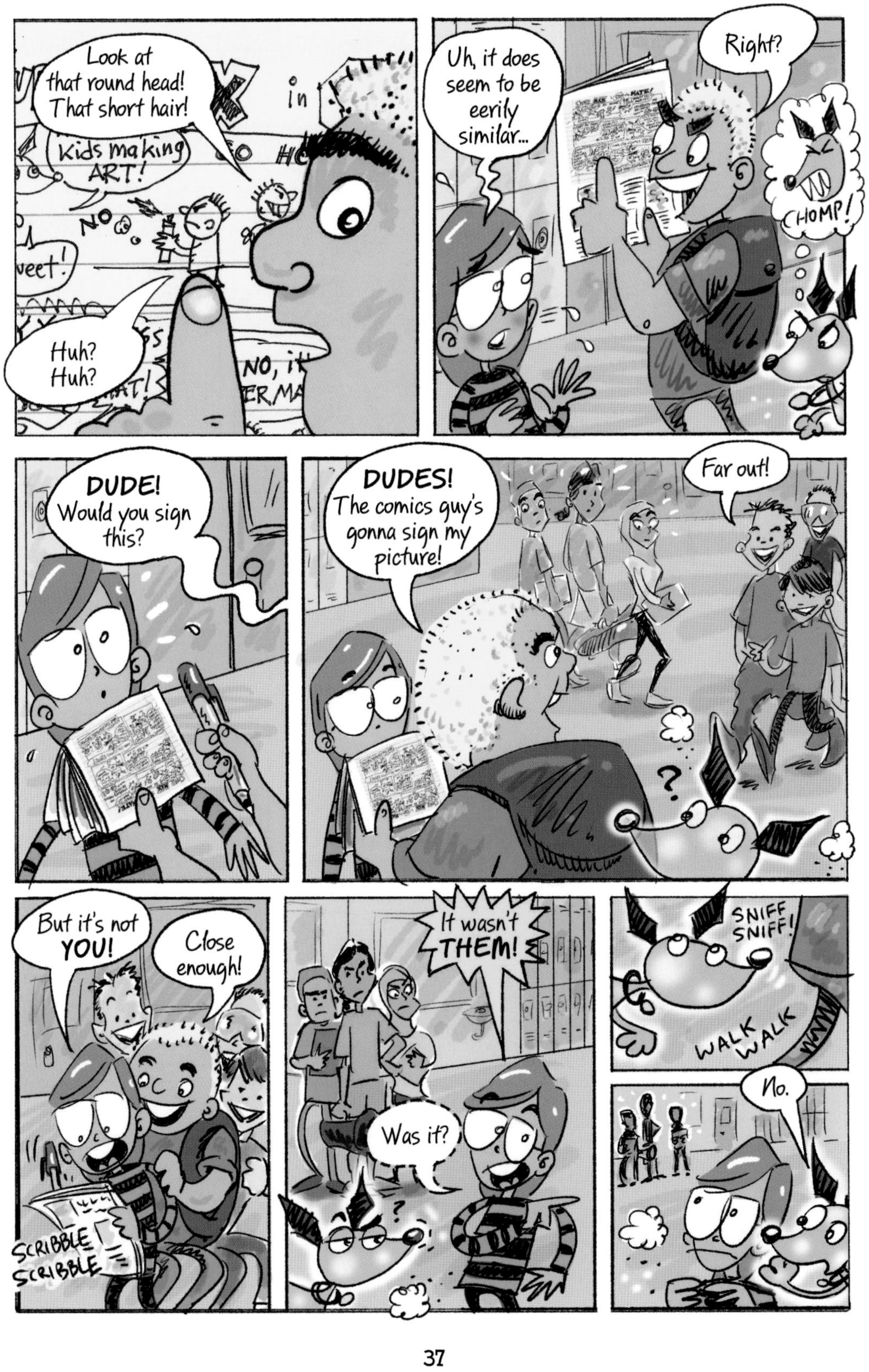
Look at that round head! That short hair!
Kids making ART!
Huh? Huh?
Uh, it does seem to be eerily similar...
Right?
CHOMP!
DUDE! Would you sign this?
DUDES! The comics guy's gonna sign my picture!
Far out!
?
But it's not YOU!
Close enough!
SCRIBBLE SCRIBBLE
It wasn't THEM!
Was it?
?
SNIFF SNIFF!
WALK WALK
No.

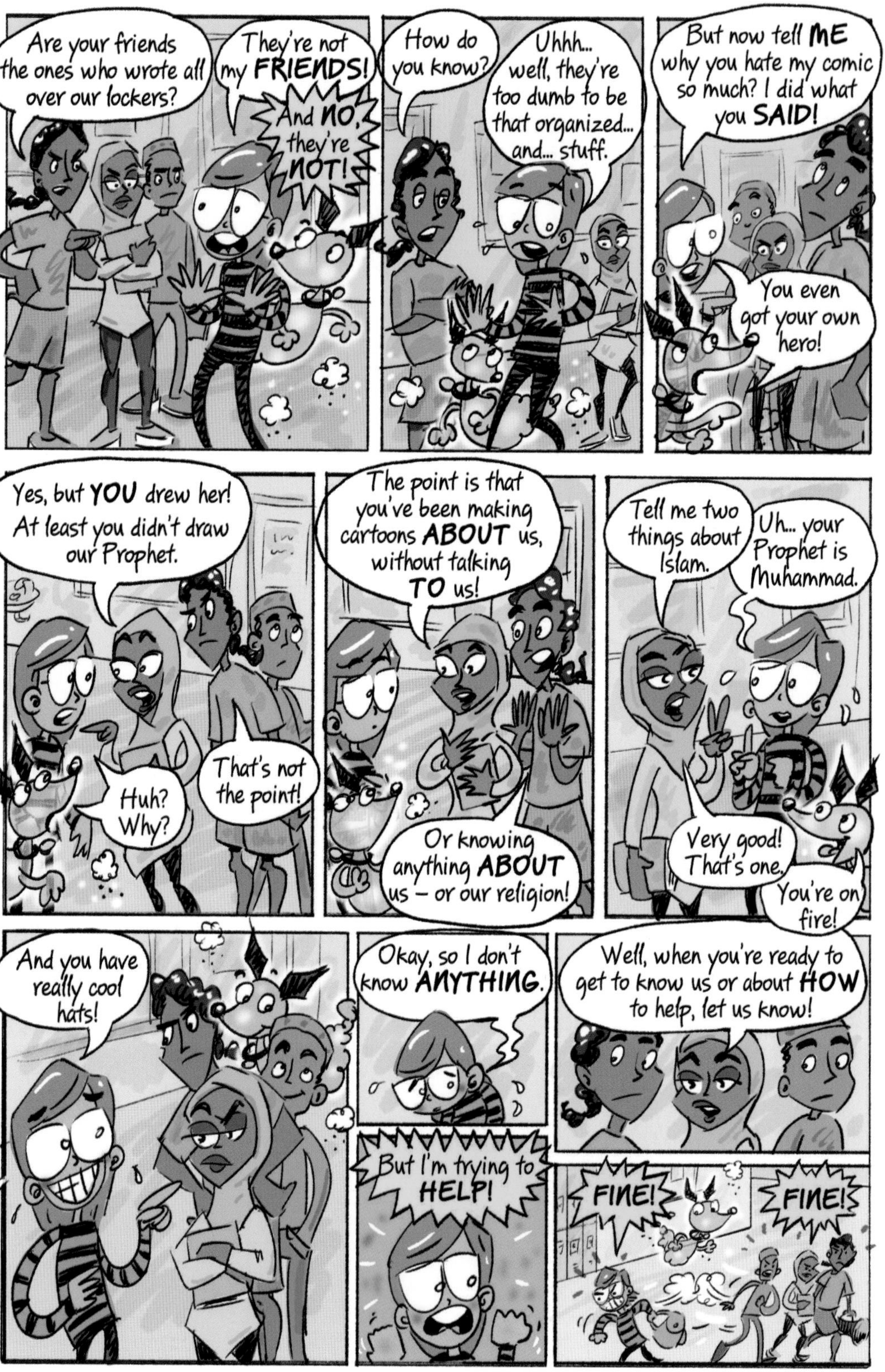
Are your friends the ones who wrote all over our lockers?
They're not my FRIENDS!
And NO, they're NOT!
How do you know?
Uhhh... well, they're too dumb to be that organized... and... stuff.
But now tell ME why you hate my comic so much? I did what you SAID!
You even got your own hero!
Yes, but YOU drew her! At least you didn't draw our Prophet.
Huh? Why?
That's not the point!
The point is that you've been making cartoons ABOUT us, without talking TO us!
Or knowing anything ABOUT us – or our religion!
Tell me two things about Islam.
Uh... your Prophet is Muhammad.
Very good! That's one.
You're on fire!
And you have really cool hats!
Okay, so I don't know ANYTHING.
But I'm trying to HELP!
Well, when you're ready to get to know us or about HOW to help, let us know!
FINE!
FINE!

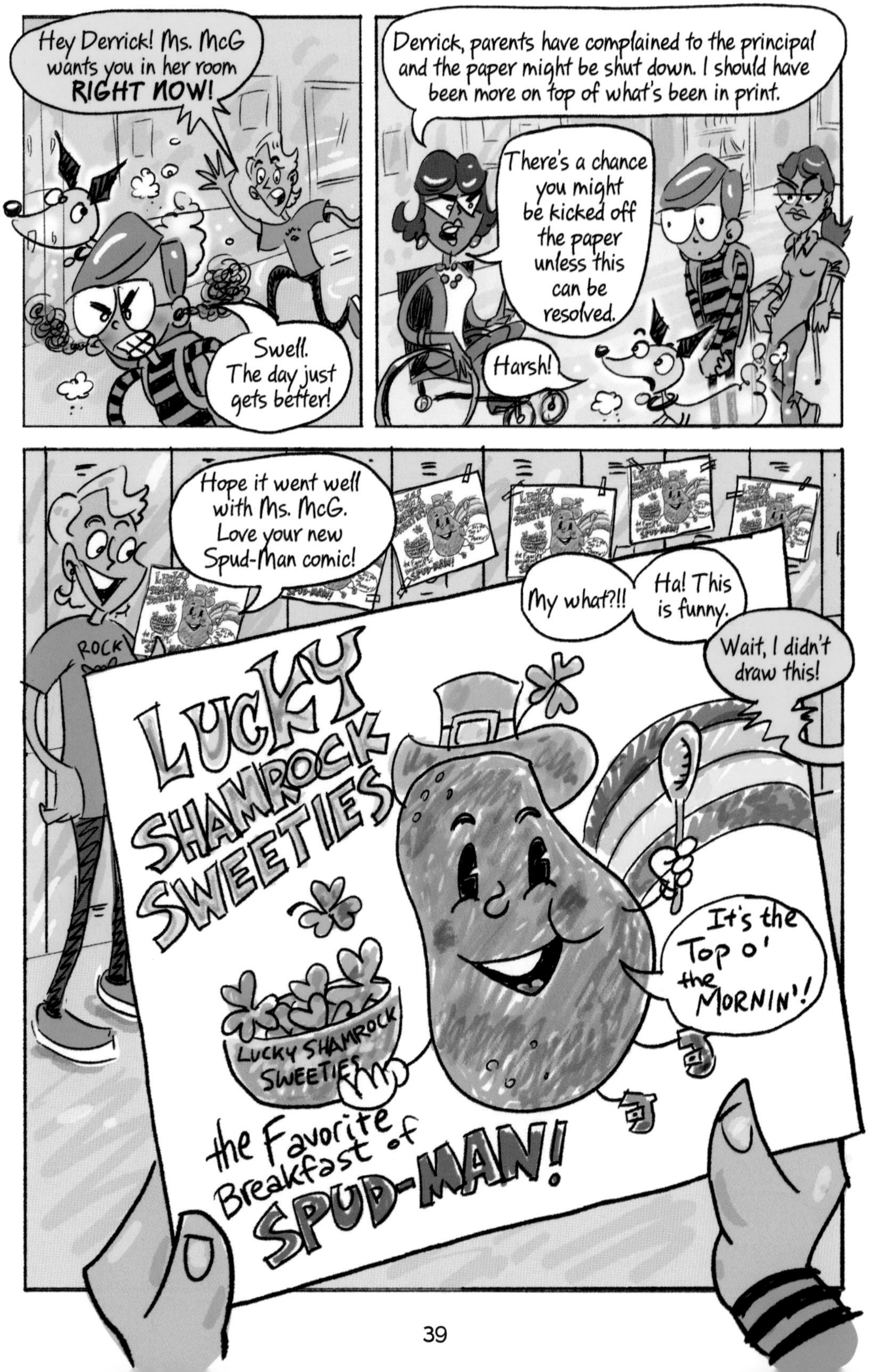
Hey Derrick! Ms. McG wants you in her room RIGHT NOW!
Swell. The day just gets better!
Derrick, parents have complained to the principal and the paper might be shut down. I should have been more on top of what's been in print.
There's a chance you might be kicked off the paper unless this can be resolved.
Harsh!
Hope it went well with Ms. McG. Love your new Spud-Man comic!
My what?!!
Ha! This is funny.
Wait, I didn't draw this!
LUCKY SHAMROCK SWEETIES
LUCKY SHAMROCK SWEETIES
the Favorite Breakfast of SPUD-MAN!
It's the Top o' the MORNIN'!
ROCK

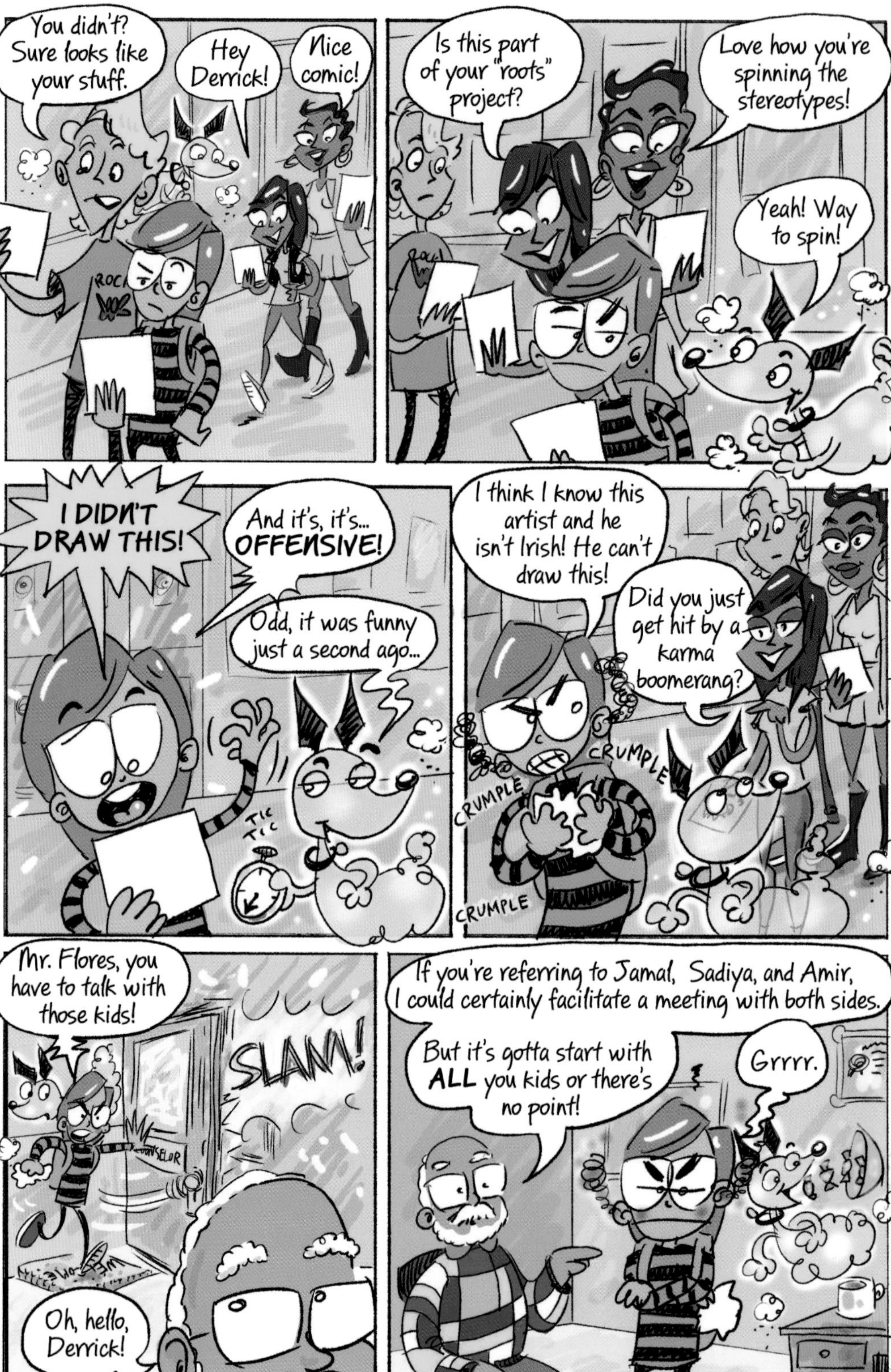
You didn't? Sure looks like your stuff.
Hey Derrick!
Nice comic!
Is this part of your "roots" project?
Love how you're spinning the stereotypes!
Yeah! Way to spin!
I DIDN'T DRAW THIS!
And it's, it's... OFFENSIVE!
Odd, it was funny just a second ago...
TIC TIC
I think I know this artist and he isn't Irish! He can't draw this!
Did you just get hit by a karma boomerang?
CRUMPLE
CRUMPLE
CRUMPLE
Mr. Flores, you have to talk with those kids!
SLAM!
Oh, hello, Derrick!
If you're referring to Jamal, Sadiya, and Amir, I could certainly facilitate a meeting with both sides.
But it's gotta start with ALL you kids or there's no point!
Grrr.

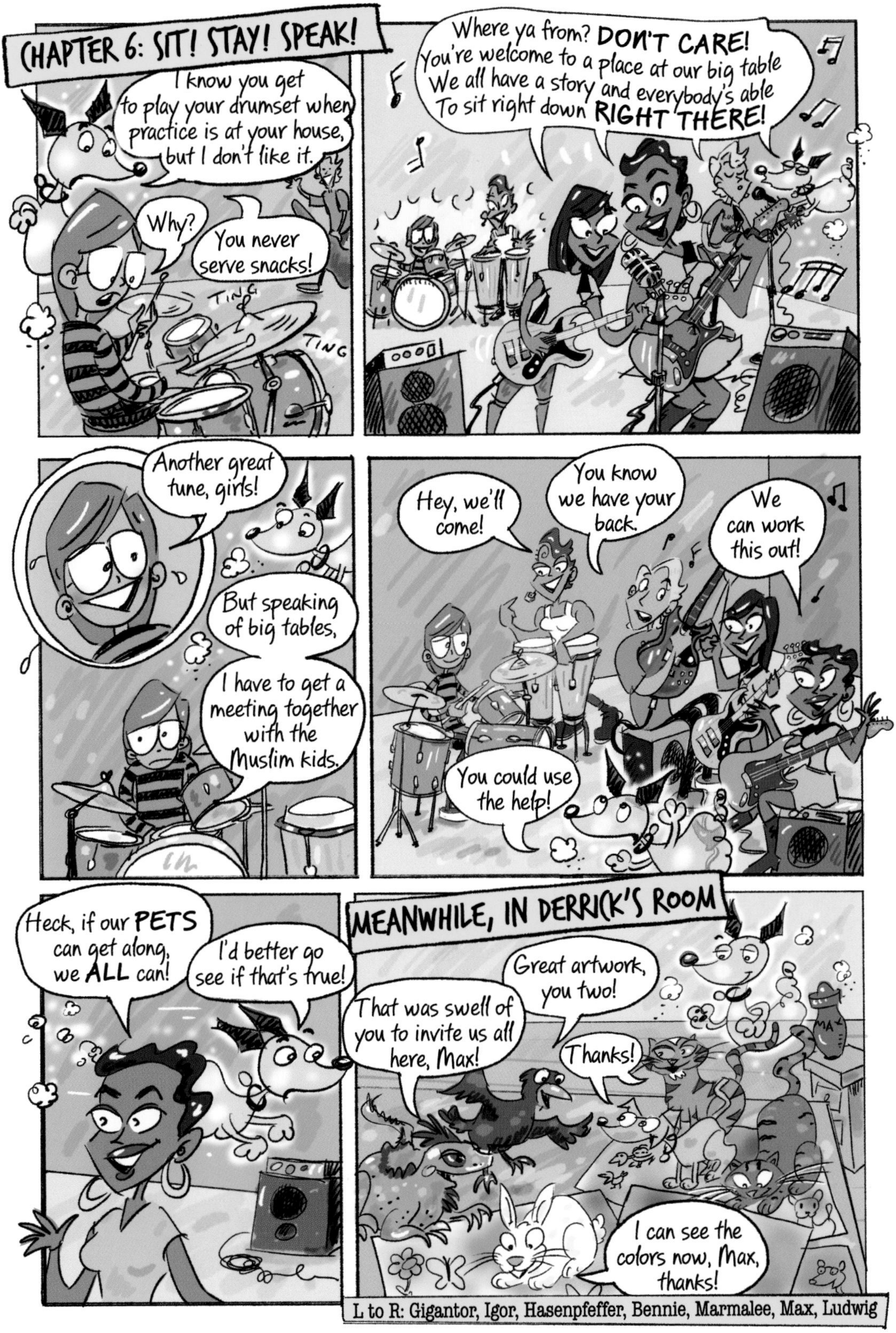
CHAPTER 6: SIT! STAY! SPEAK!
I know you get to play your drumset when practice is at your house, but I don't like it.
Why?
You never serve snacks!
TING
TING
Where ya from? DON'T CARE! You're welcome to a place at our big table We all have a story and everybody's able To sit right down RIGHT THERE!
Another great tune, girls!
But speaking of big tables,
I have to get a meeting together with the Muslim kids.
Hey, we'll come!
You know we have your back.
We can work this out!
You could use the help!
Heck, if our PETS can get along, we ALL can!
I'd better go see if that's true!
MEANWHILE, IN DERRICK'S ROOM
Great artwork, you two!
That was swell of you to invite us all here, Max!
Thanks!
I can see the colors now, Max, thanks!
L to R: Gigantor, Igor, Hasenpfeffer, Bennie, Marmalee, Max, Ludwig

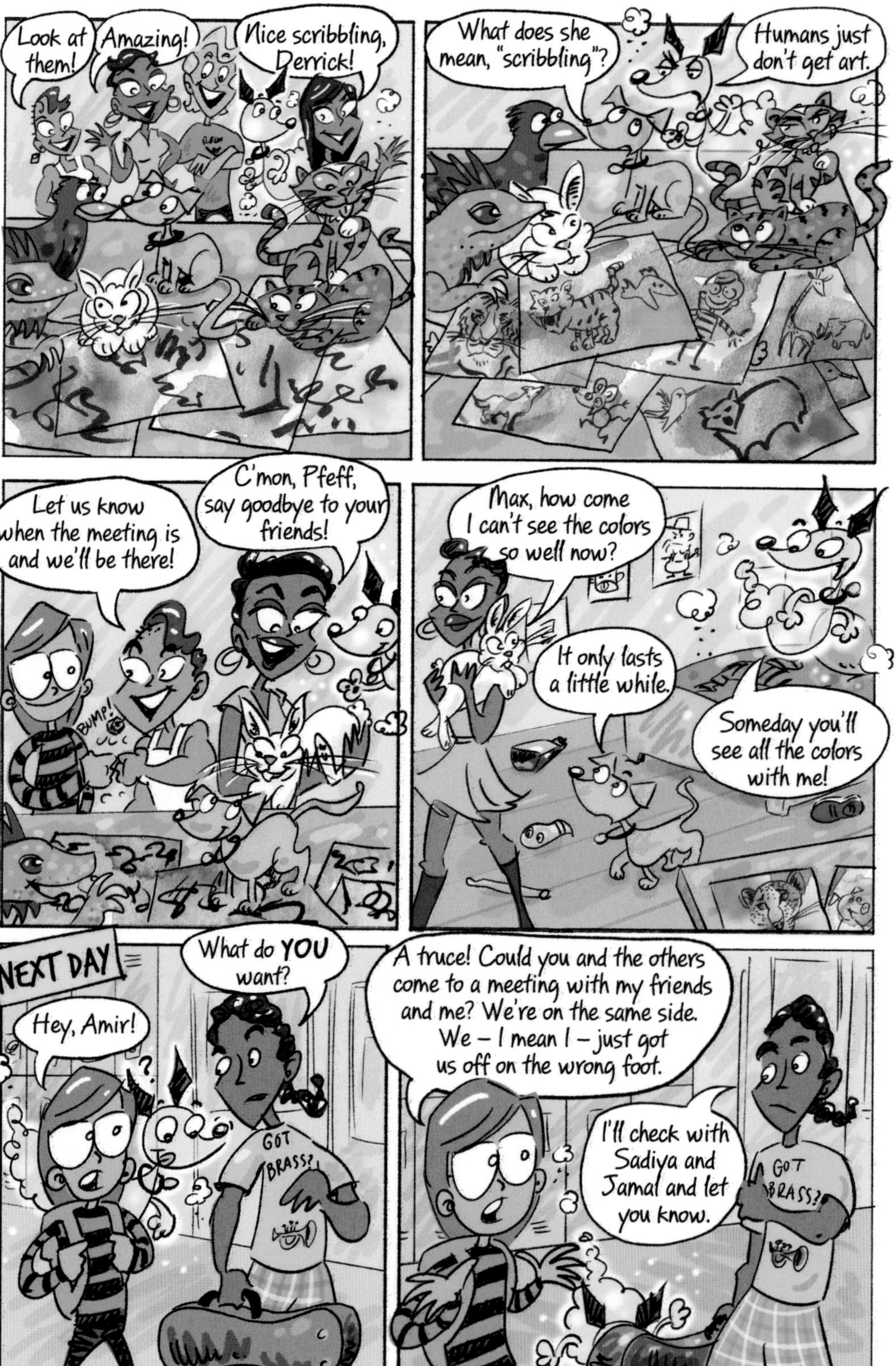
Look at them!
Amazing!
Nice scribbling, Derrick!
What does she mean, "scribbling"?
Humans just don't get art.
Let us know when the meeting is and we'll be there!
C'mon, Pfeff, say goodbye to your friends!
BUMP!
Max, how come I can't see the colors so well now?
It only lasts a little while.
Someday you'll see all the colors with me!
NEXT DAY
Hey, Amir!
What do YOU want?
GOT BRASS?
A truce! Could you and the others come to a meeting with my friends and me? We're on the same side. We – I mean I – just got us off on the wrong foot.
I'll check with Sadiya and Jamal and let you know.
GOT BRASS?

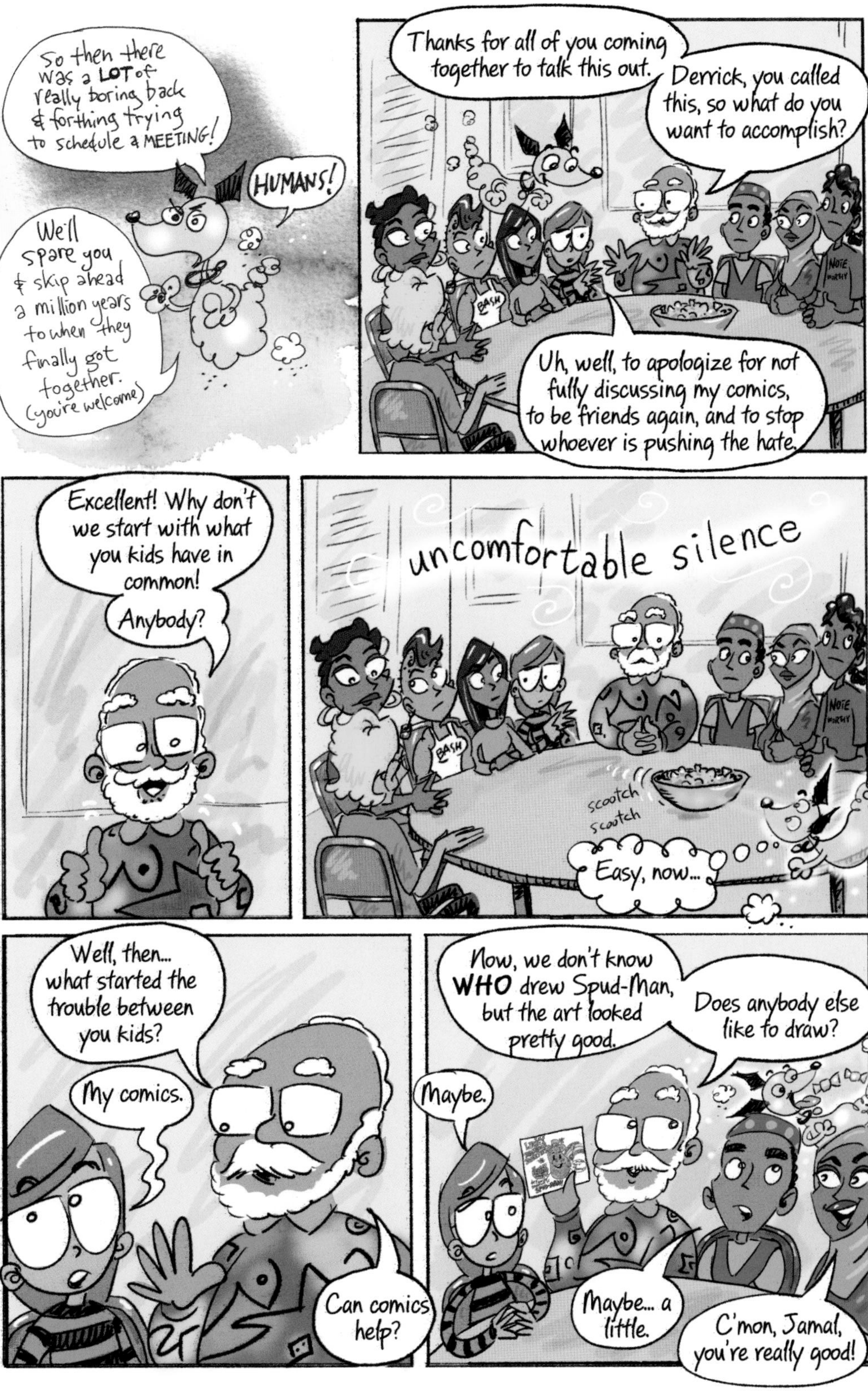
So then there was a LOT of really boring back & forthing trying to schedule a MEETING!
HUMANS!
We'll spare you & skip ahead a million years to when they finally got together. (you're welcome)
Thanks for all of you coming together to talk this out.
Derrick, you called this, so what do you want to accomplish?
Uh, well, to apologize for not fully discussing my comics, to be friends again, and to stop whoever is pushing the hate.
Excellent! Why don't we start with what you kids have in common!
Anybody?
uncomfortable silence
scootch
scootch
Easy, now...
Well, then... what started the trouble between you kids?
My comics.
Can comics help?
Now, we don't know WHO drew Spud-Man, but the art looked pretty good.
Does anybody else like to draw?
Maybe.
Maybe... a little.
C'mon, Jamal, you're really good!

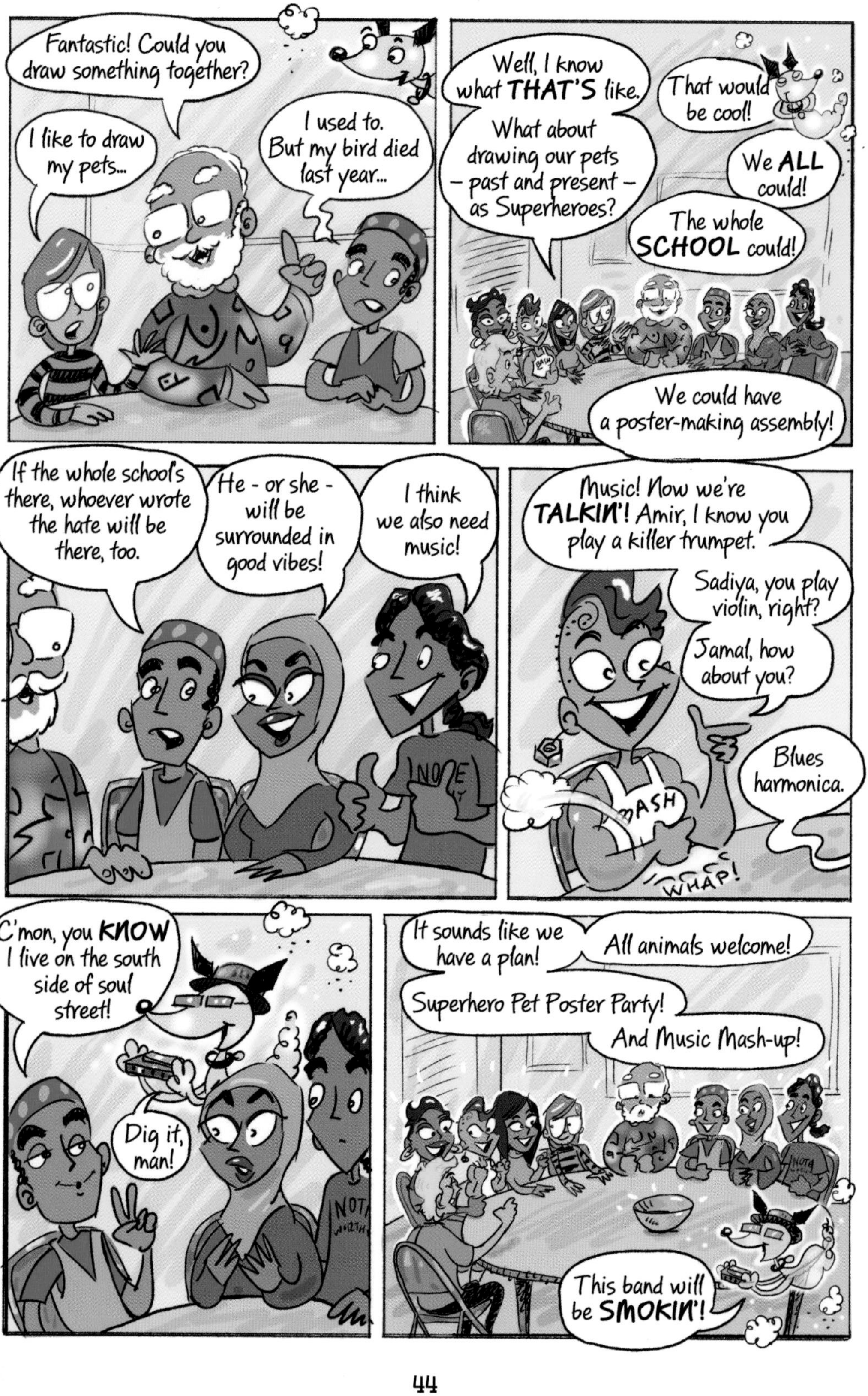
Fantastic! Could you draw something together?
I like to draw my pets...
I used to. But my bird died last year...
Well, I know what THAT'S like.
What about drawing our pets – past and present – as Superheroes?
That would be cool!
We ALL could!
The whole SCHOOL could!
We could have a poster-making assembly!
If the whole school's there, whoever wrote the hate will be there, too.
He - or she - will be surrounded in good vibes!
I think we also need music!
Music! Now we're TALKIN'! Amir, I know you play a killer trumpet.
Sadiya, you play violin, right?
Jamal, how about you?
Blues harmonica.
MASH
WHAP!
C'mon, you KNOW I live on the south side of soul street!
Dig it, man!
NOT
It sounds like we have a plan!
All animals welcome!
Superhero Pet Poster Party!
And Music Mash-up!
This band will be SMOKIN'!

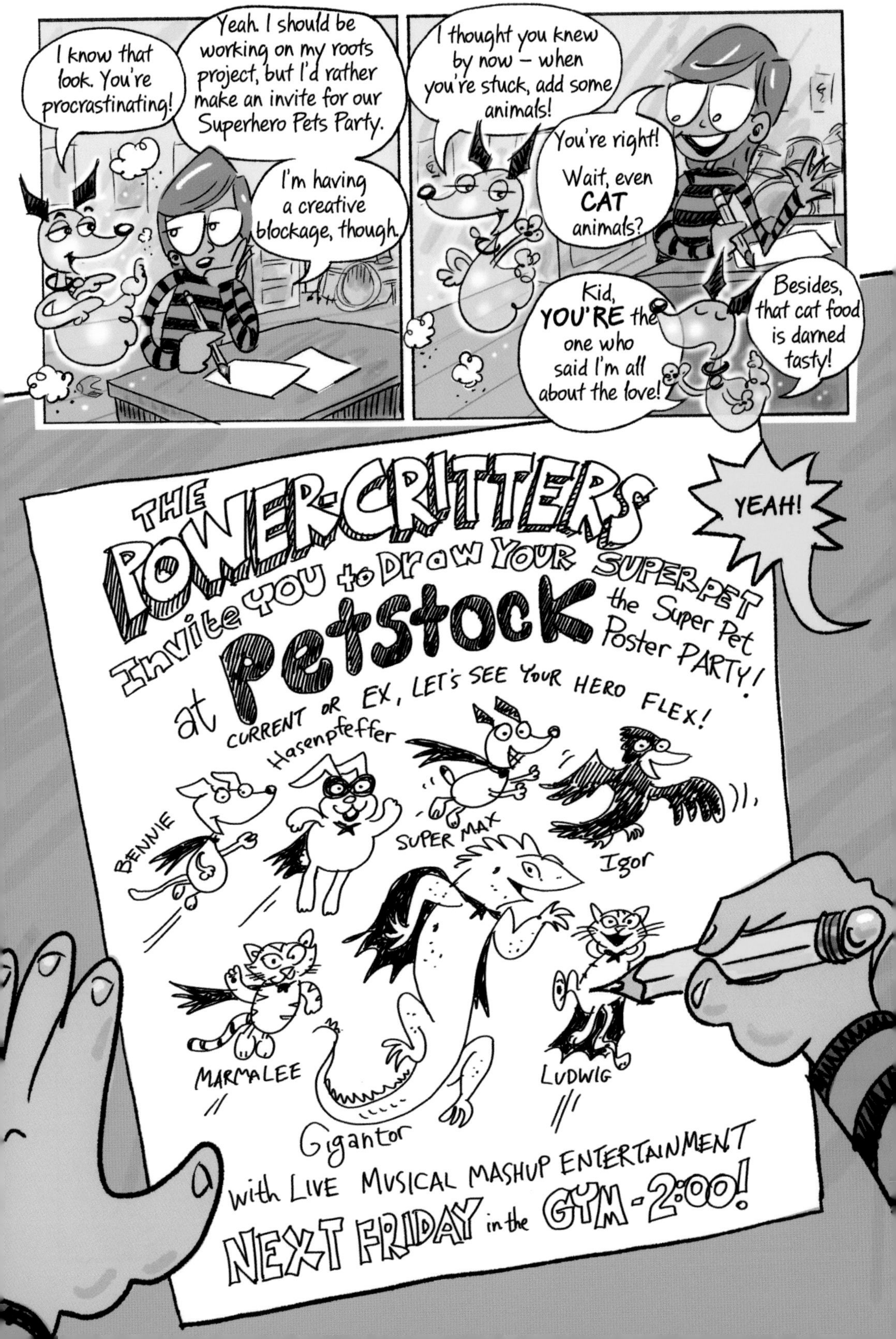

I know that look. You're procrastinating!
Yeah. I should be working on my roots project, but I'd rather make an invite for our Superhero Pets Party.
I'm having a creative blockage, though.
I thought you knew by now — when you're stuck, add some animals!
You're right!
Wait, even CAT animals?
Kid, YOU'RE the one who said I'm all about the love!
Besides, that cat food is darned tasty!
YEAH!
THE POWER-CRITTERS Invite YOU to Draw YOUR SUPERPET at Petstock the Super Pet Poster PARTY!
CURRENT OR EX, LET'S SEE YOUR HERO FLEX!
Hasenpfeffer
BENNIE
SUPER MAX
Igor
MARMALEE
LUDWIG
Gigantor
with LIVE MUSICAL MASHUP ENTERTAINMENT
NEXT FRIDAY in the GYM-2:00!

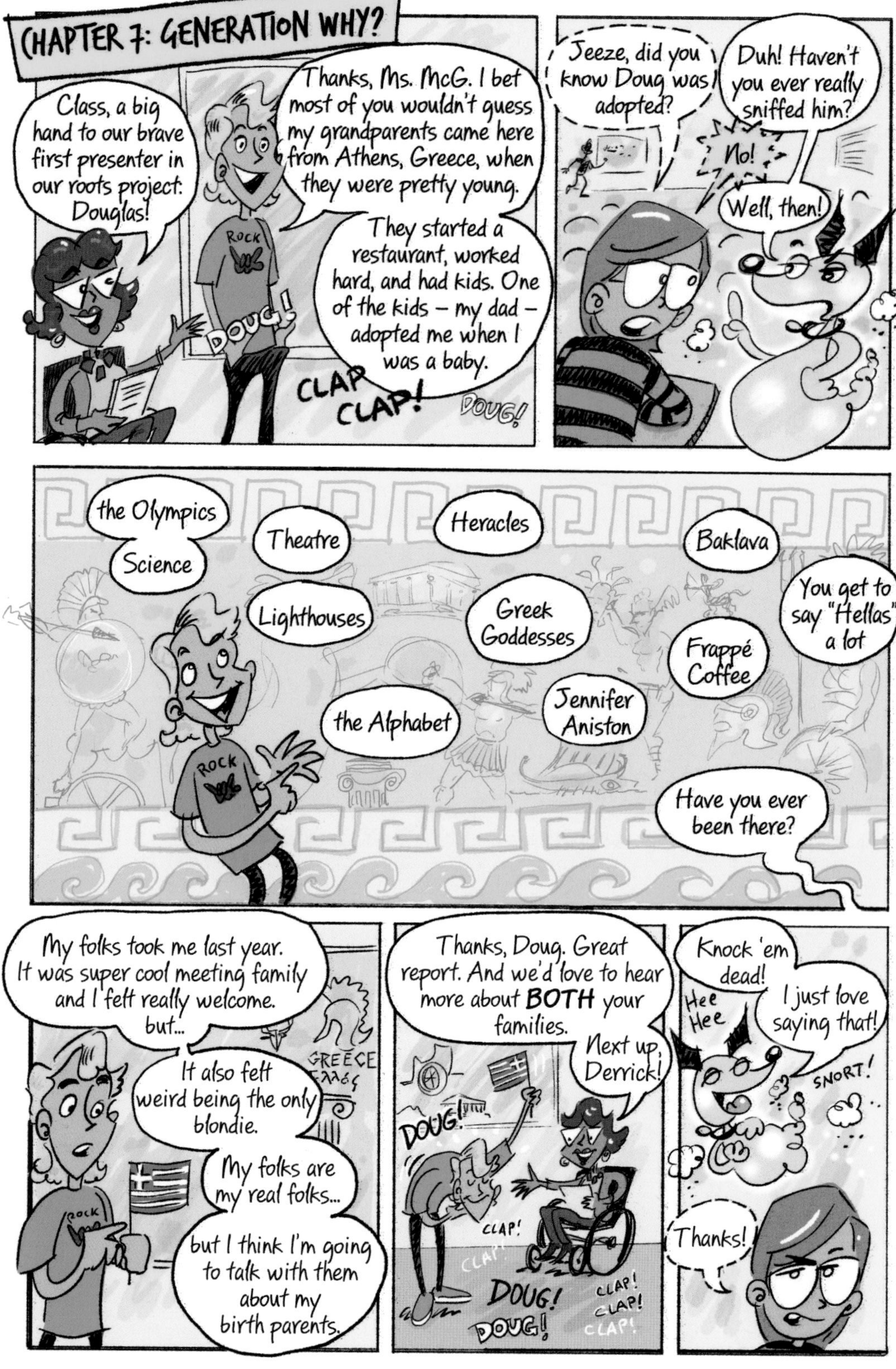
CHAPTER 7: GENERATION WHY?
Class, a big hand to our brave first presenter in our roots project. Douglas!
Thanks, Ms. McG. I bet most of you wouldn't guess my grandparents came here from Athens, Greece, when they were pretty young.
They started a restaurant, worked hard, and had kids. One of the kids – my dad – adopted me when I was a baby.
DOUG!
CLAP CLAP!
DOUG!
Jeeze, did you know Doug was adopted?
Duh! Haven't you ever really sniffed him?
No!
Well, then!
the Olympics
Science
Theatre
Lighthouses
Heracles
Greek Goddesses
the Alphabet
Jennifer Aniston
Baklava
Frappé Coffee
You get to say "Hellas" a lot
Have you ever been there?
My folks took me last year. It was super cool meeting family and I felt really welcome. but...
It also felt weird being the only blondie.
My folks are my real folks...
but I think I'm going to talk with them about my birth parents.
Thanks, Doug. Great report. And we'd love to hear more about BOTH your families.
Next up, Derrick!
DOUG!
CLAP!
CLAP!
DOUG!
DOUG!
CLAP! CLAP! CLAP!
Knock 'em dead!
I just love saying that!
Hee Hee
SNORT!
Thanks!

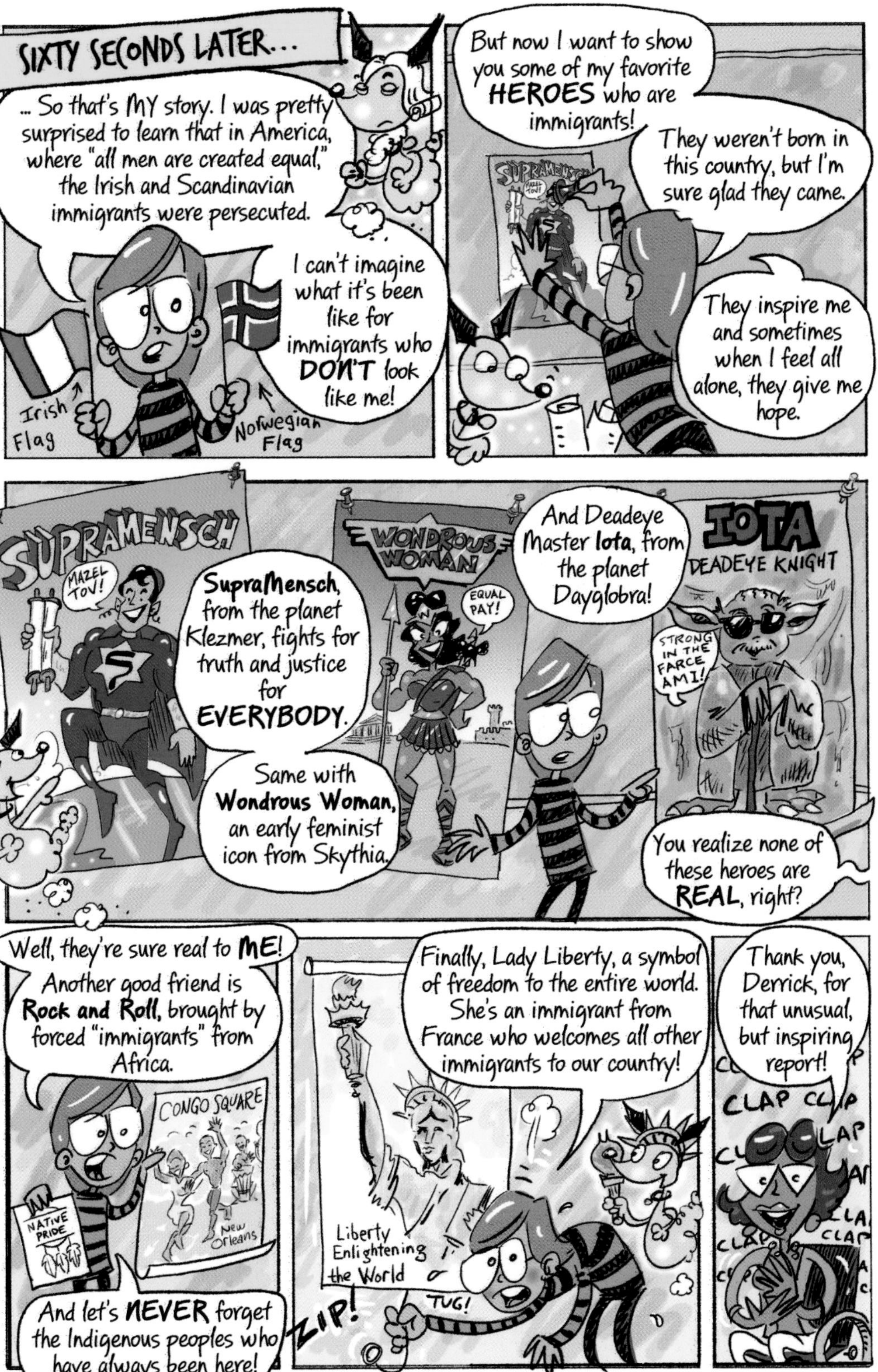

SIXTY SECONDS LATER...
... So that's MY story. I was pretty surprised to learn that in America, where "all men are created equal," the Irish and Scandinavian immigrants were persecuted.
I can't imagine what it's been like for immigrants who DON'T look like me!
Irish Flag
Norwegian Flag
But now I want to show you some of my favorite HEROES who are immigrants!
They weren't born in this country, but I'm sure glad they came.
They inspire me and sometimes when I feel all alone, they give me hope.
SUPRAMENSCH
MAZEL TOV!
SupraMensch, from the planet Klezmer, fights for truth and justice for EVERYBODY.
WONDROUS WOMAN
EQUAL PAY!
Same with Wondrous Woman, an early feminist icon from Skythia.
And Deadeye Master Iota, from the planet Dayglobra!
IOTA
DEADEYE KNIGHT
STRONG IN THE FARCE AMI!
You realize none of these heroes are REAL, right?
Well, they're sure real to ME! Another good friend is Rock and Roll, brought by forced "immigrants" from Africa.
CONGO SQUARE
New Orleans
NATIVE PRIDE
And let's NEVER forget the Indigenous peoples who have always been here!
ZIP!
Finally, Lady Liberty, a symbol of freedom to the entire world. She's an immigrant from France who welcomes all other immigrants to our country!
Liberty Enlightening the World
TUG!
Thank you, Derrick, for that unusual, but inspiring report!
CLAP CLAP

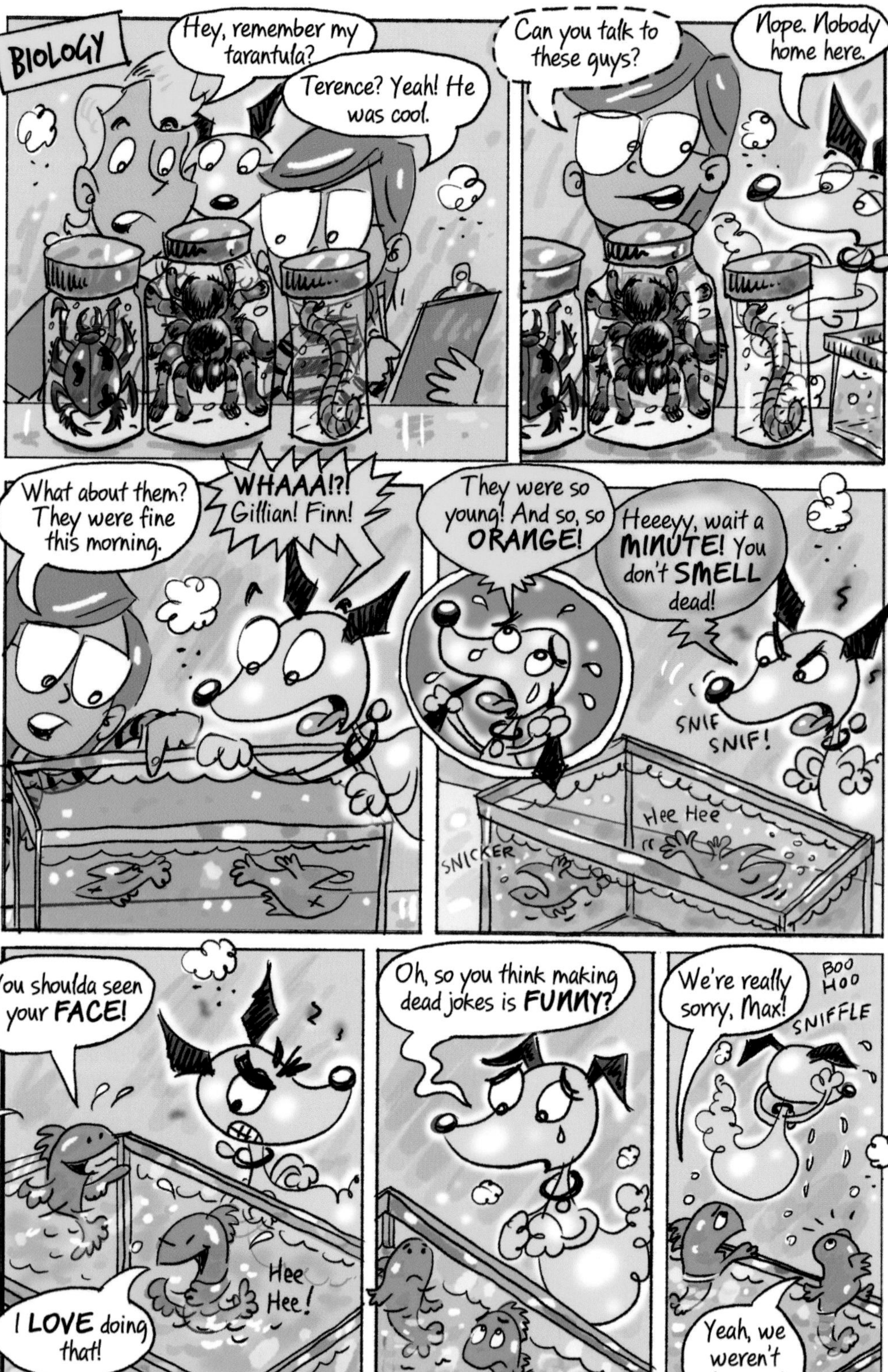
BIOLOGY
Hey, remember my tarantula?
Terence? Yeah! He was cool.
Can you talk to these guys?
Nope. Nobody home here.
What about them? They were fine this morning.
WHAAA!?! Gillian! Finn!
They were so young! And so, so ORANGE!
Heeeyy, wait a MINUTE! You don't SMELL dead!
SNIF SNIF!
Hee Hee
SNICKER
You shoulda seen your FACE!
I LOVE doing that!
Hee Hee!
Oh, so you think making dead jokes is FUNNY?
We're really sorry, Max!
BOO HOO
SNIFFLE
Yeah, we weren't thinking!

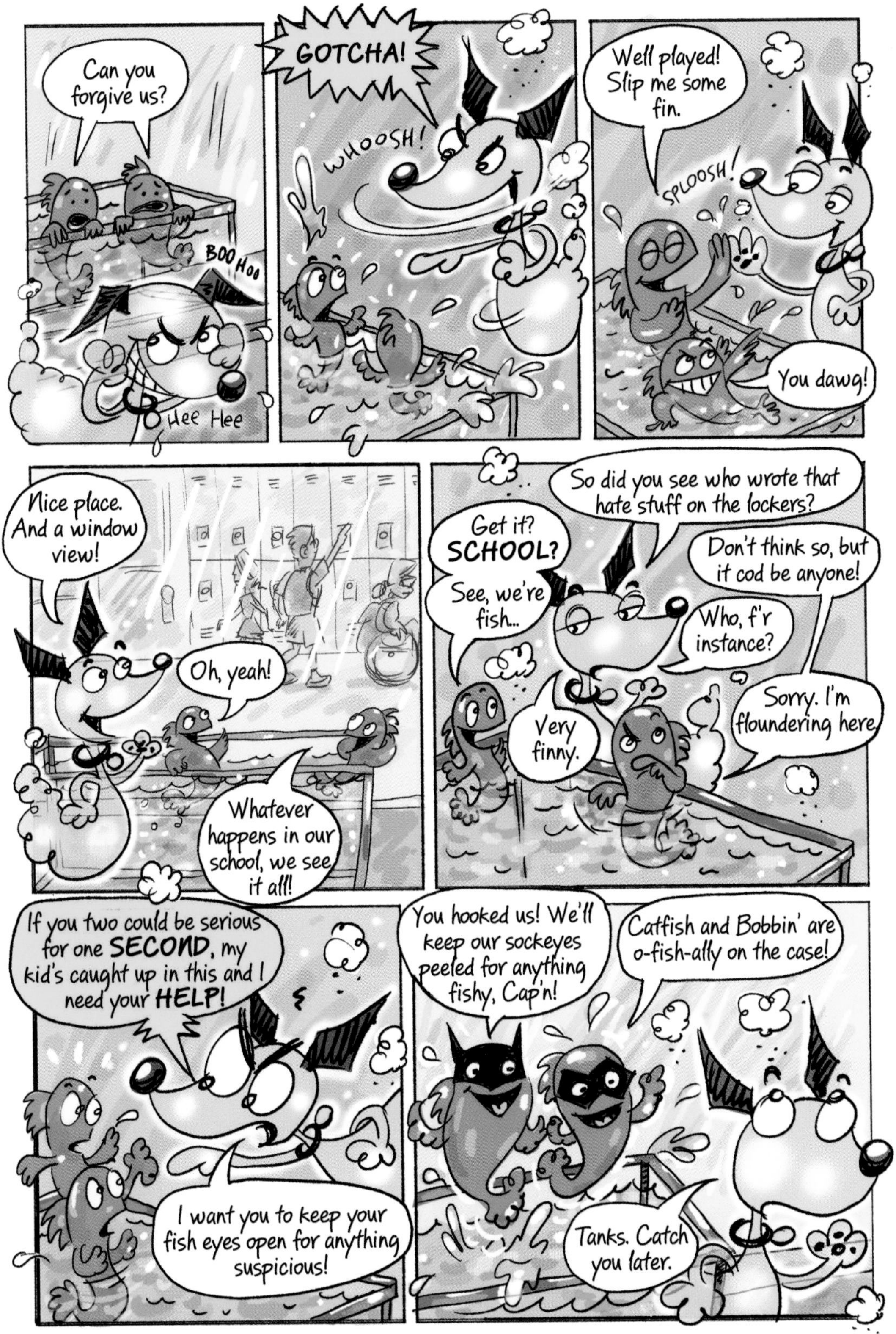

Can you forgive us?
BOO HOO
Hee Hee
GOTCHA!
WHOOSH!
Well played! Slip me some fin.
SPLOOSH!
You dawg!
Nice place. And a window view!
Oh, yeah!
Whatever happens in our school, we see it all!
Get it? SCHOOL?
See, we're fish...
So did you see who wrote that hate stuff on the lockers?
Don't think so, but it cod be anyone!
Who, f'r instance?
Very finny.
Sorry. I'm floundering here.
If you two could be serious for one SECOND, my kid's caught up in this and I need your HELP!
I want you to keep your fish eyes open for anything suspicious!
You hooked us! We'll keep our sockeyes peeled for anything fishy, Cap'n!
Catfish and Bobbin' are o-fish-ally on the case!
Tanks. Catch you later.

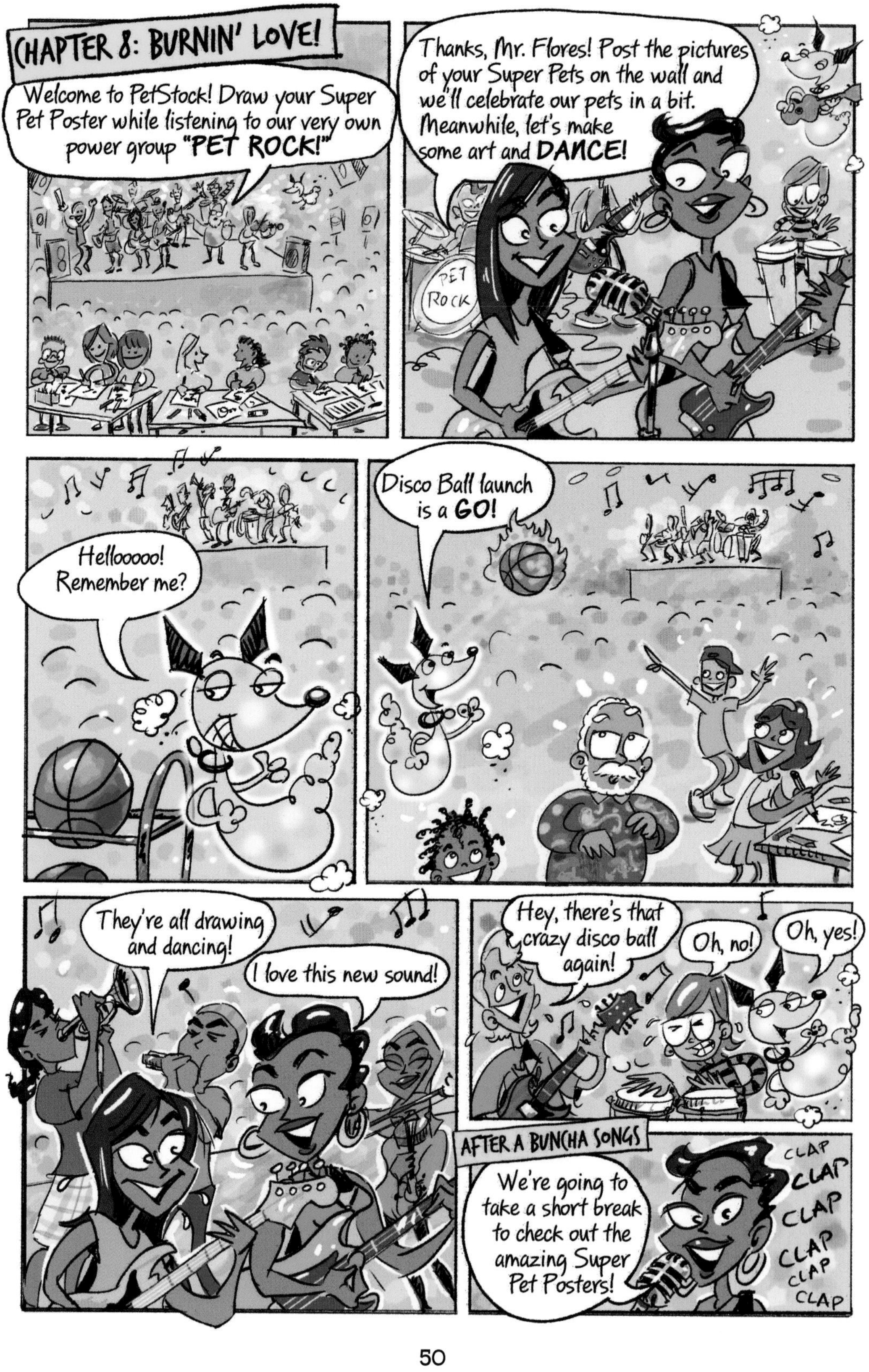
CHAPTER 8: BURNIN' LOVE!
Welcome to PetStock! Draw your Super Pet Poster while listening to our very own power group "PET ROCK!"
Thanks, Mr. Flores! Post the pictures of your Super Pets on the wall and we'll celebrate our pets in a bit. Meanwhile, let's make some art and DANCE!
PET ROCK
Hellooooo! Remember me?
Disco Ball launch is a GO!
They're all drawing and dancing!
I love this new sound!
Hey, there's that crazy disco ball again!
Oh, no!
Oh, yes!
AFTER A BUNCHA SONGS
We're going to take a short break to check out the amazing Super Pet Posters!
CLAP CLAP CLAP CLAP CLAP CLAP

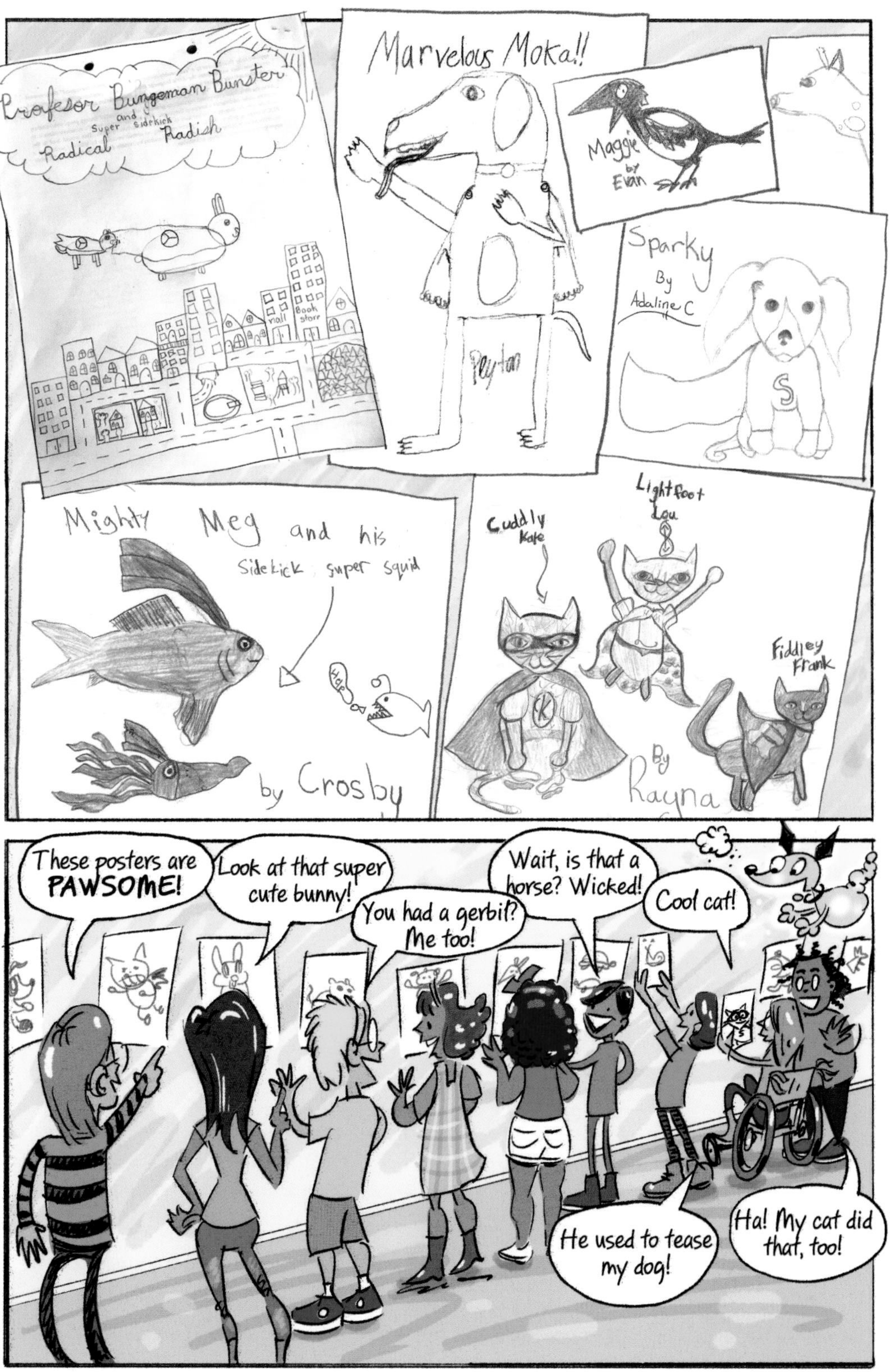
Profesor Bungeman Bunster
and super sidekick Radical Radish
Marvelous Moka!!
Peyton
Maggie by Evan
Sparky
By Adaline C
Mighty Meg and his
sidekick super squid
by Crosby
Lightfoot Lou
Cuddly Kate
Fiddley Frank
By Rayna
These posters are PAWSOME!
Look at that super cute bunny!
You had a gerbil? Me too!
Wait, is that a horse? Wicked!
Cool cat!
He used to tease my dog!
Ha! My cat did that, too!

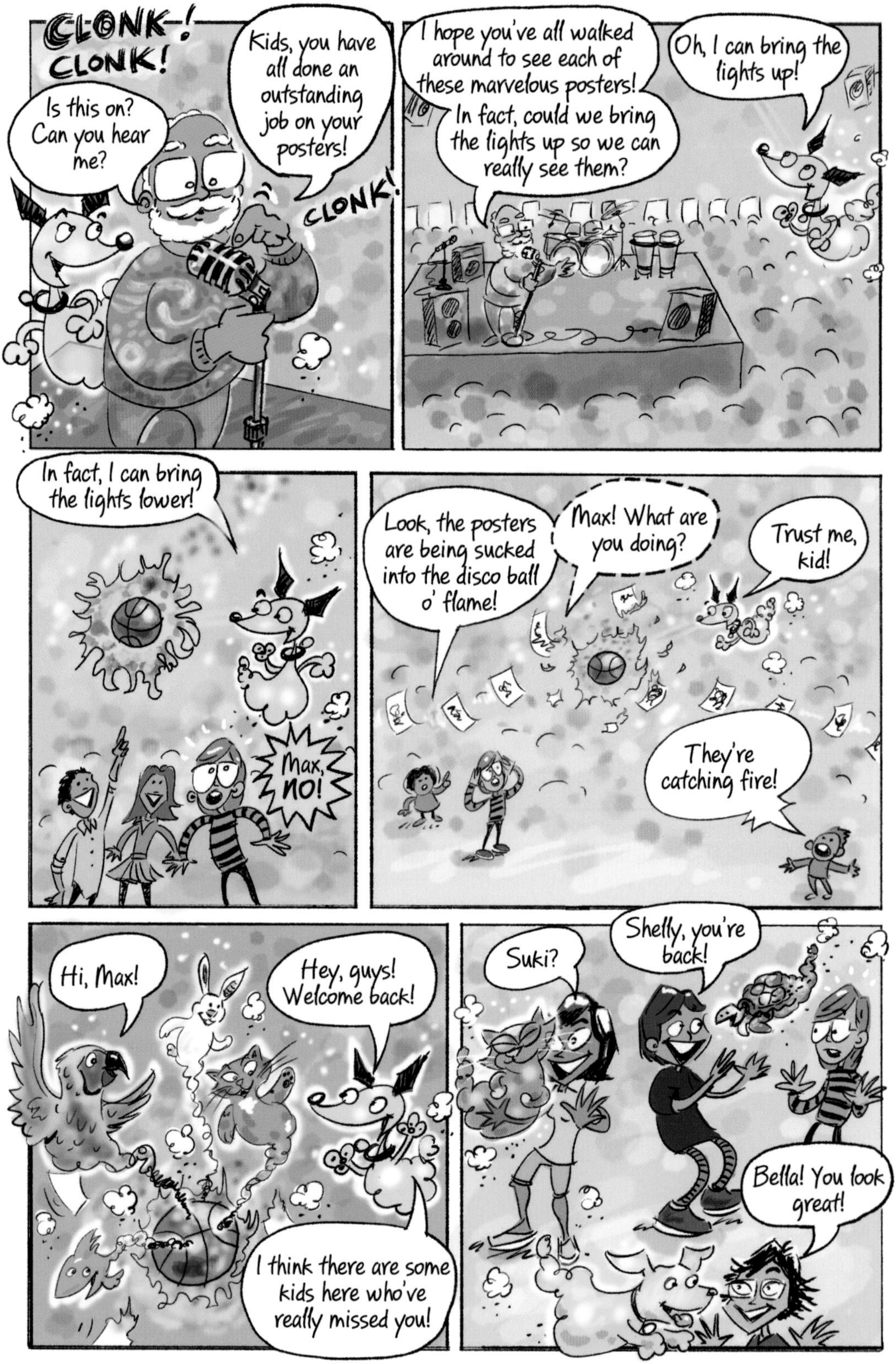

CLONK! CLONK!
Is this on? Can you hear me?
Kids, you have all done an outstanding job on your posters!
CLONK!
I hope you've all walked around to see each of these marvelous posters!
In fact, could we bring the lights up so we can really see them?
Oh, I can bring the lights up!
In fact, I can bring the lights lower!
Max, NO!
Look, the posters are being sucked into the disco ball o' flame!
Max! What are you doing?
Trust me, kid!
They're catching fire!
Hi, Max!
Hey, guys! Welcome back!
I think there are some kids here who've really missed you!
Suki?
Shelly, you're back!
Bella! You look great!

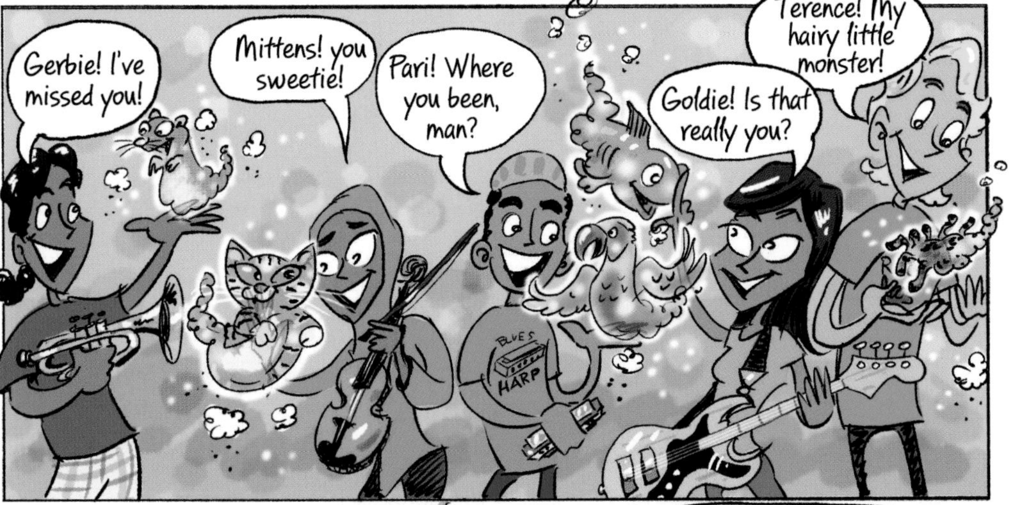
Gerbie! I've missed you!
Mittens! you sweetie!
Pari! Where you been, man?
Goldie! Is that really you?
Terence! My hairy little monster!
BLUES HARP

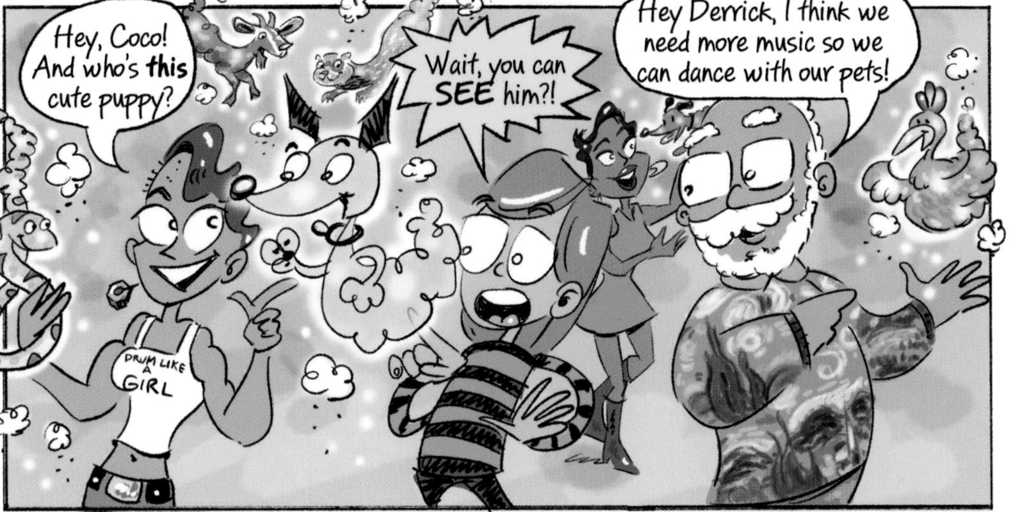
Hey, Coco! And who's **this** cute puppy?
Wait, you can **SEE** him?!
Hey Derrick, I think we need more music so we can dance with our pets!
DRUM LIKE A GIRL

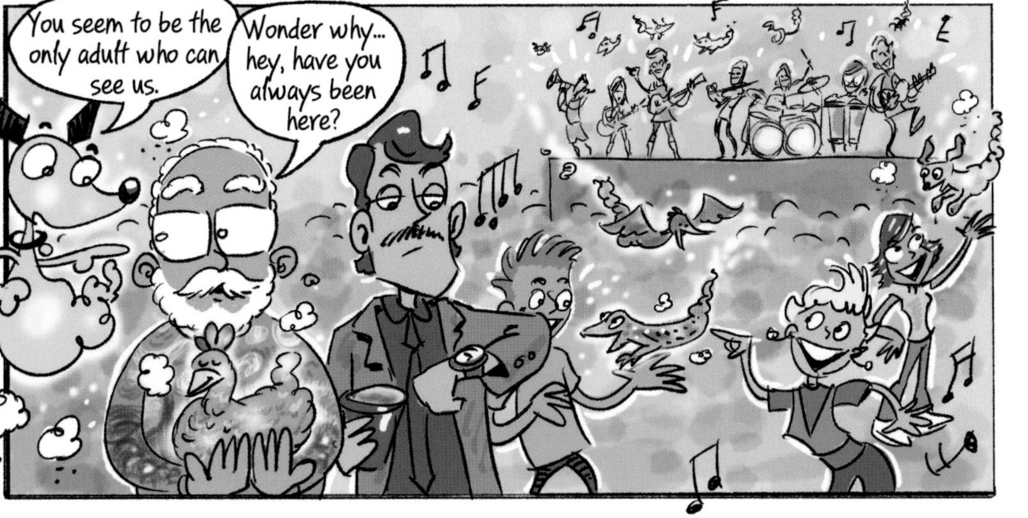
You seem to be the only adult who can see us.
Wonder why... hey, have you always been here?

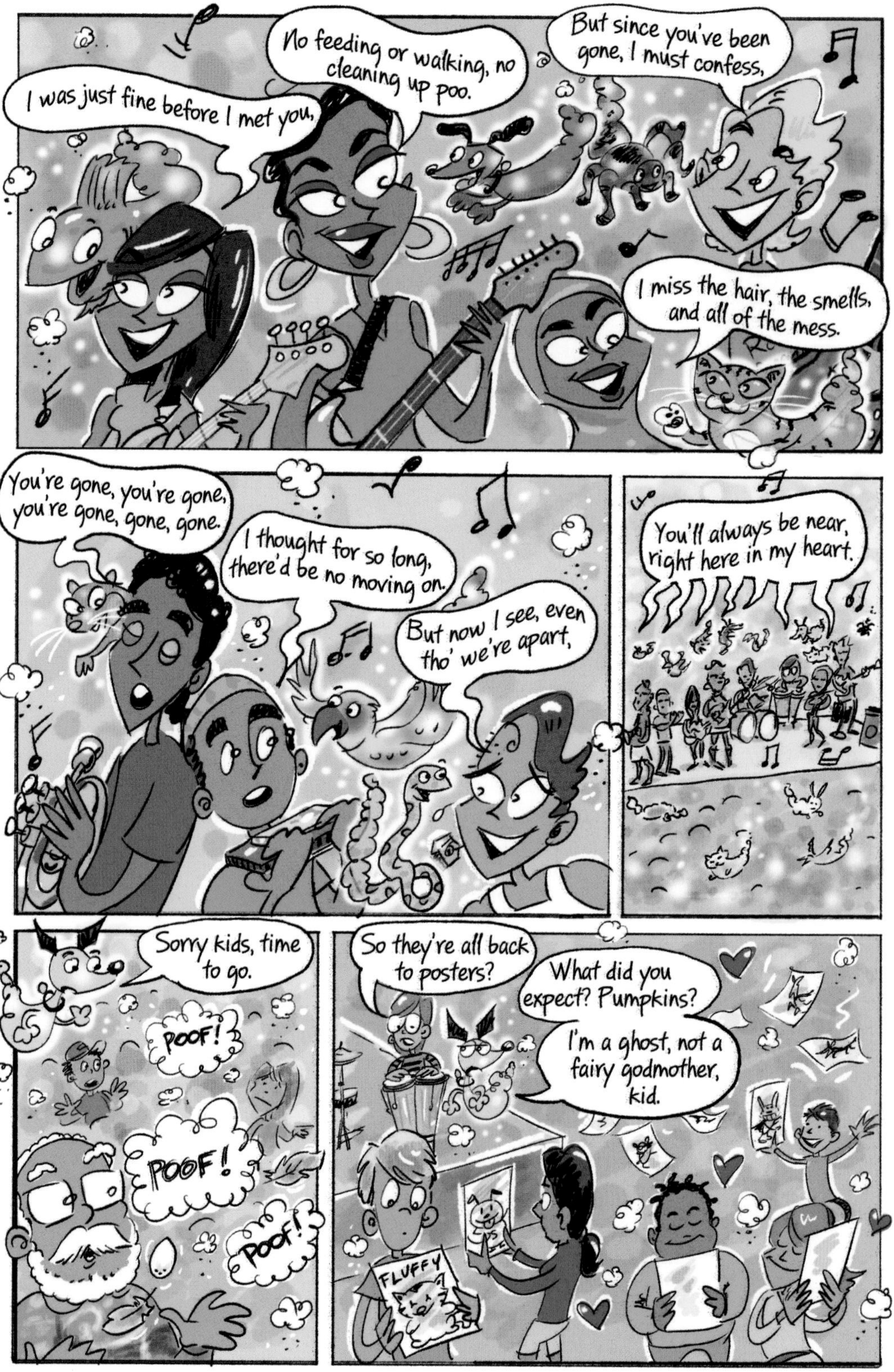
I was just fine before I met you,
No feeding or walking, no cleaning up poo.
But since you've been gone, I must confess,
I miss the hair, the smells, and all of the mess.
You're gone, you're gone, you're gone, gone, gone.
I thought for so long, there'd be no moving on.
But now I see, even tho' we're apart,
You'll always be near, right here in my heart.
Sorry kids, time to go.
POOF!
POOF!
POOF!
So they're all back to posters?
What did you expect? Pumpkins?
I'm a ghost, not a fairy godmother, kid.
FLUFFY

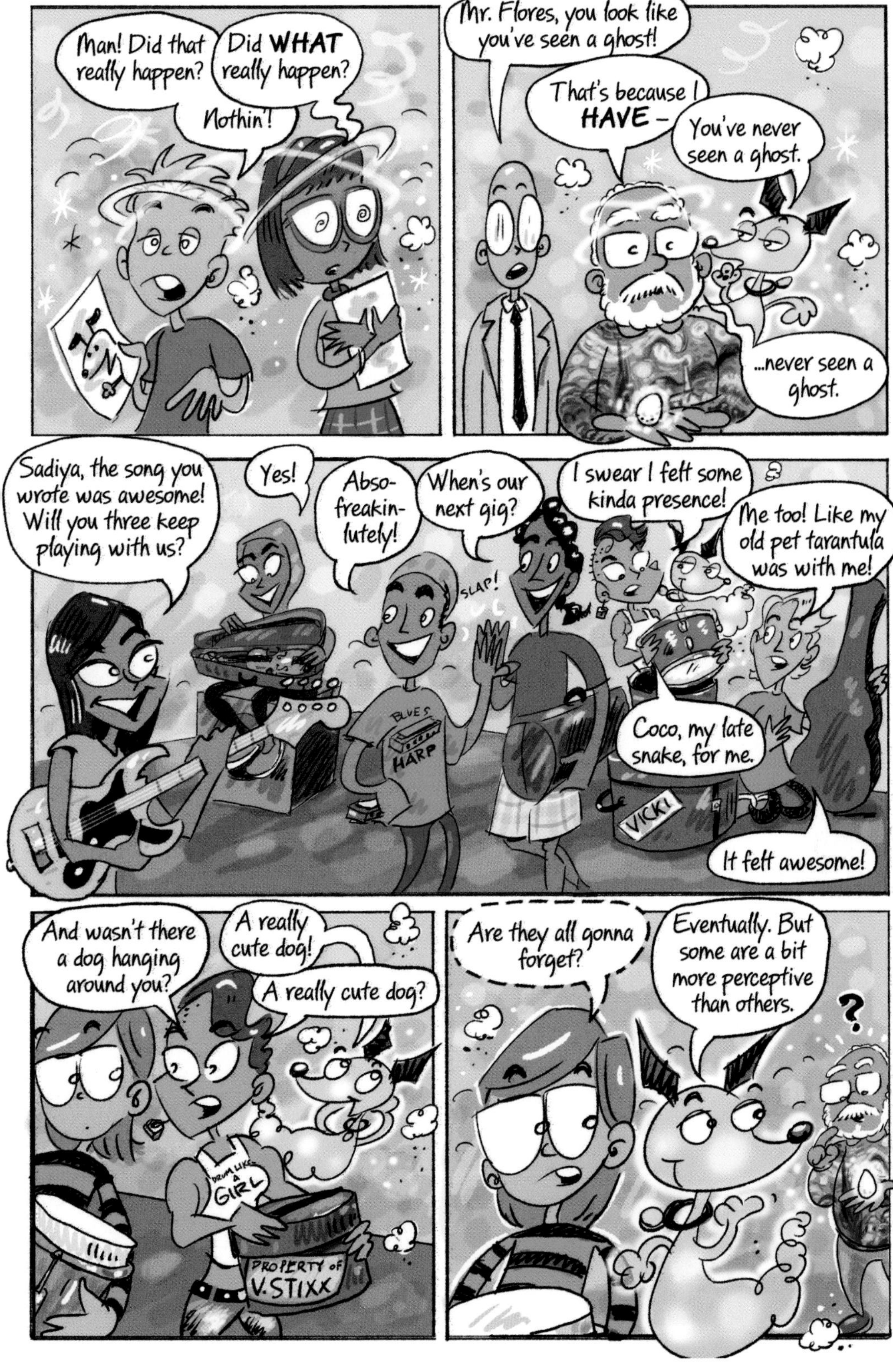

Man! Did that really happen?
Did WHAT really happen?
Nothin'!
Mr. Flores, you look like you've seen a ghost!
That's because I HAVE –
You've never seen a ghost.
...never seen a ghost.
Sadiya, the song you wrote was awesome! Will you three keep playing with us?
Yes!
Abso-freakin-lutely!
When's our next gig?
SLAP!
I swear I felt some kinda presence!
Me too! Like my old pet tarantula was with me!
Coco, my late snake, for me.
It felt awesome!
BLUES HARP
VICKI
And wasn't there a dog hanging around you?
A really cute dog!
A really cute dog?
DRUM LIKE A GIRL
PROPERTY OF V. STIXX
Are they all gonna forget?
Eventually. But some are a bit more perceptive than others.
?

CHAPTER 9: FRIENDS FUR-EVER!

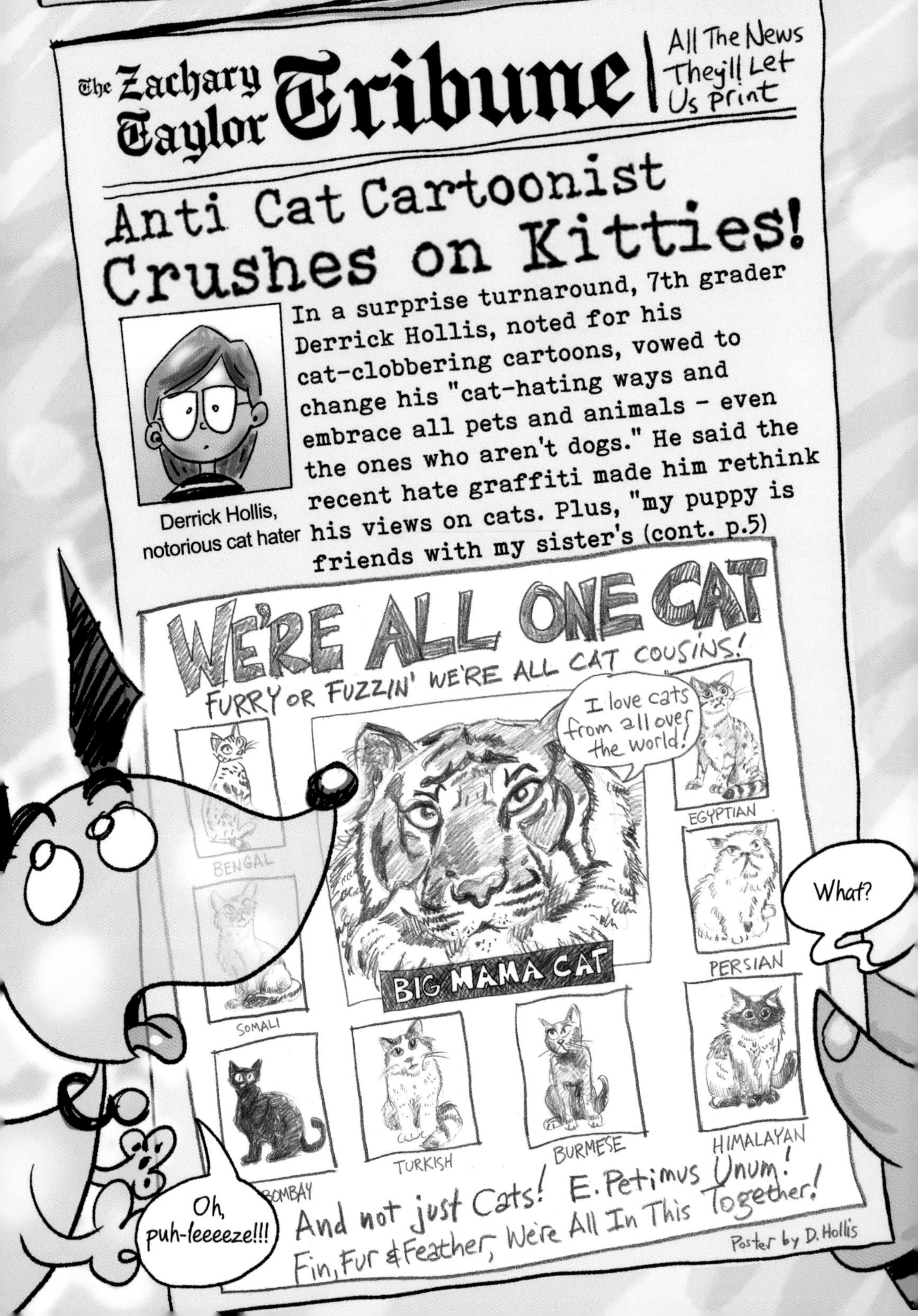

The Zachary Taylor Tribune
All The News They'll Let Us Print
Anti Cat Cartoonist Crushes on Kitties!
In a surprise turnaround, 7th grader Derrick Hollis, noted for his cat-clobbering cartoons, vowed to change his "cat-hating ways and embrace all pets and animals - even the ones who aren't dogs." He said the recent hate graffiti made him rethink his views on cats. Plus, "my puppy is friends with my sister's (cont. p.5)
Derrick Hollis, notorious cat hater
WE'RE ALL ONE CAT
WE'RE ALL CAT COUSINS!
FURRY OR FUZZIN'
I love cats from all over the world!
BENGAL
EGYPTIAN
PERSIAN
BIG MAMA CAT
SOMALI
BOMBAY
TURKISH
BURMESE
HIMALAYAN
What?
And not just Cats! E. Petimus Unum!
Fin, Fur & Feather, We're All In This Together!
Poster by D. Hollis
Oh, puh-leeeeze!!!

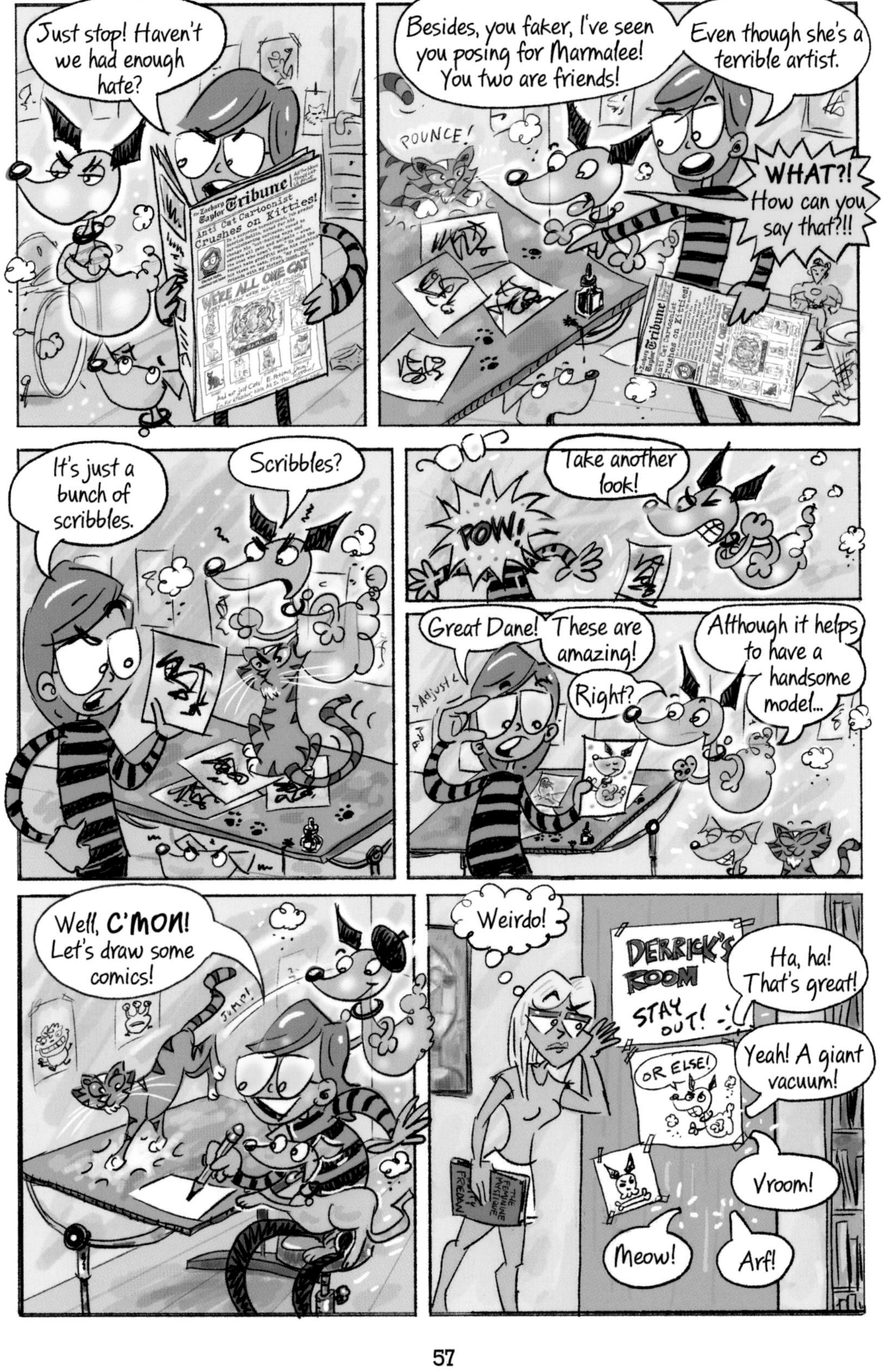
Just stop! Haven't we had enough hate?
Zachary Taylor Tribune
Anti Cat Cartoonist Crushes on Kitties!
WE'RE ALL ONE CAT
Besides, you faker, I've seen you posing for Marmalee! You two are friends!
Even though she's a terrible artist.
POUNCE!
WHAT?! How can you say that?!!
It's just a bunch of scribbles.
Scribbles?
POW!
Take another look!
Great Dane!
These are amazing!
Adjust
Right?
Although it helps to have a handsome model...
Well, C'MON! Let's draw some comics!
JUMP!
Weirdo!
DERRICK'S ROOM
STAY OUT!
OR ELSE!
Ha, ha! That's great!
Yeah! A giant vacuum!
FRIEDAN
THE FEMININE MYSTIQUE
Vroom!
Meow!
Arf!

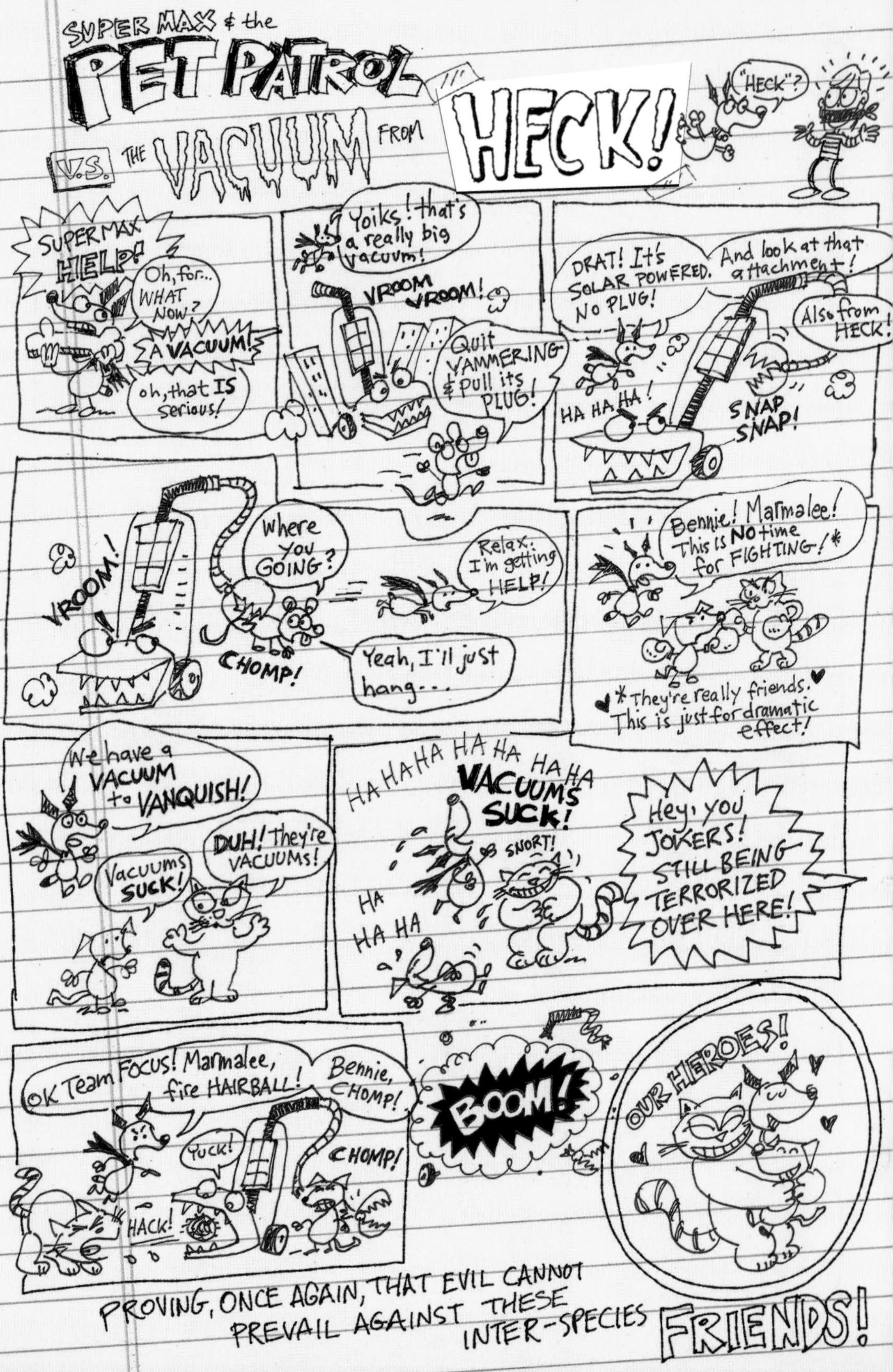
SUPER MAX & the
PET PATROL
V.S. THE VACUUM FROM HECK!
"HECK"?
SUPER MAX HELP!
Oh, for... WHAT NOW?
A VACUUM!
oh, that IS serious!
Yoiks! that's a really big vacuum!
VROOM VROOM!
Quit YAMMERING & pull its PLUG!
DRAT! It's SOLAR POWERED. NO PLUG!
And look at that attachment!
Also from HECK!
HA HA HA!
SNAP SNAP!
VROOM!
Where you GOING?
CHOMP!
Relax. I'm getting HELP!
Yeah, I'll just hang...
Bennie! Marmalee! This is NO time for FIGHTING!*
* They're really friends. This is just for dramatic effect!
We have a VACUUM to VANQUISH!
Vacuums SUCK!
DUH! They're VACUUMS!
HA HA HA HA HA HA HA
VACUUMS SUCK!
SNORT!
HA HA HA
Hey, you JOKERS! STILL BEING TERRORIZED OVER HERE!
OK Team FOCUS! Marmalee, fire HAIRBALL!
Bennie, CHOMP!
YUCK!
CHOMP!
HACK!
BOOM!
OUR HEROES!
PROVING, ONCE AGAIN, THAT EVIL CANNOT PREVAIL AGAINST THESE INTER-SPECIES FRIENDS!

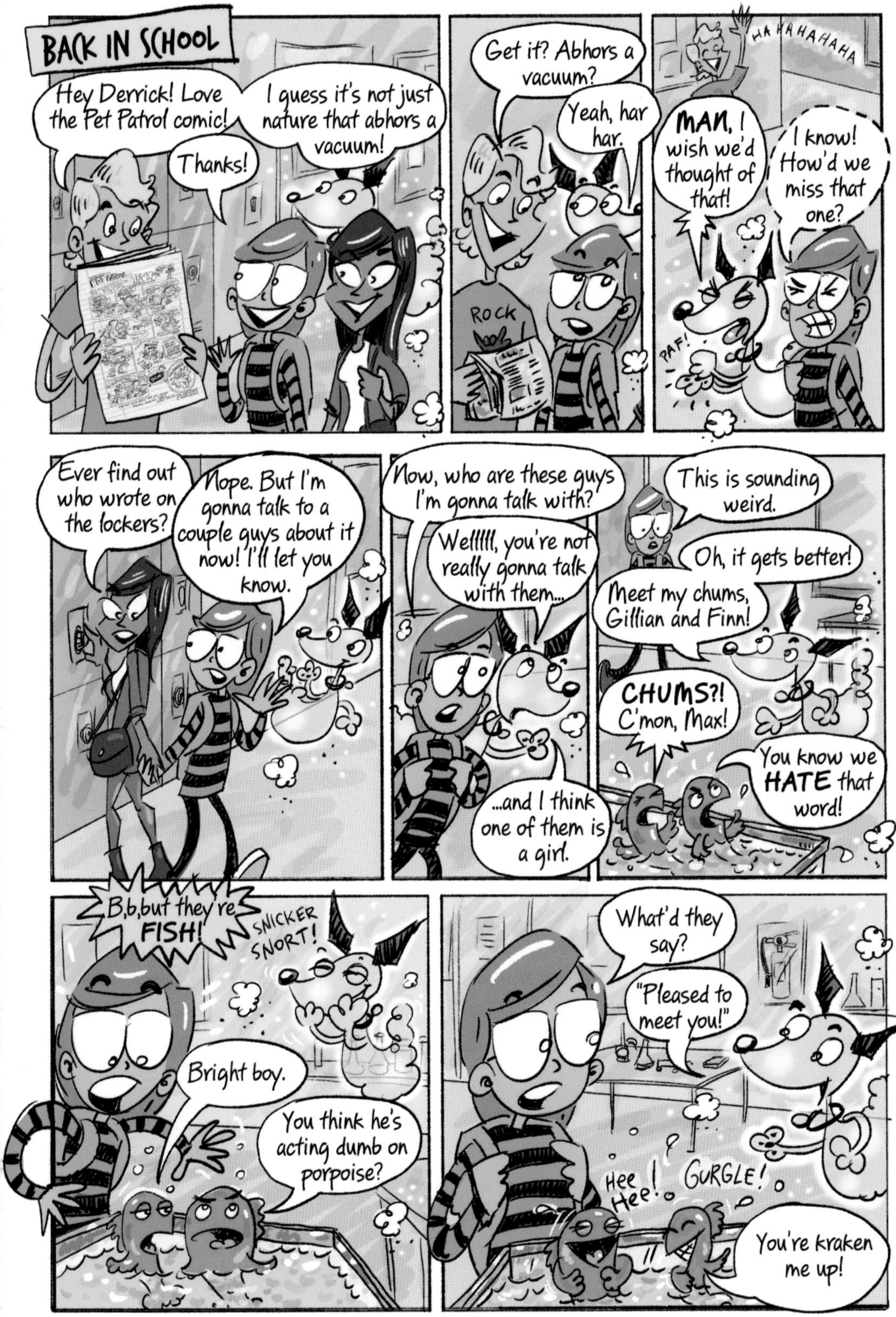
BACK IN SCHOOL
Hey Derrick! Love the Pet Patrol comic!
Thanks!
I guess it's not just nature that abhors a vacuum!
Get it? Abhors a vacuum?
Yeah, har har.
HAHAHAHAHAHA
MAN, I wish we'd thought of that!
I know! How'd we miss that one?
PAF!
Ever find out who wrote on the lockers?
Nope. But I'm gonna talk to a couple guys about it now! I'll let you know.
Now, who are these guys I'm gonna talk with?
Welllll, you're not really gonna talk with them...
...and I think one of them is a girl.
This is sounding weird.
Oh, it gets better!
Meet my chums, Gillian and Finn!
CHUMS?! C'mon, Max!
You know we HATE that word!
B,b,but they're FISH!
SNICKER SNORT!
Bright boy.
You think he's acting dumb on porpoise?
What'd they say?
"Pleased to meet you!"
Hee Hee!
GURGLE!
You're kraken me up!

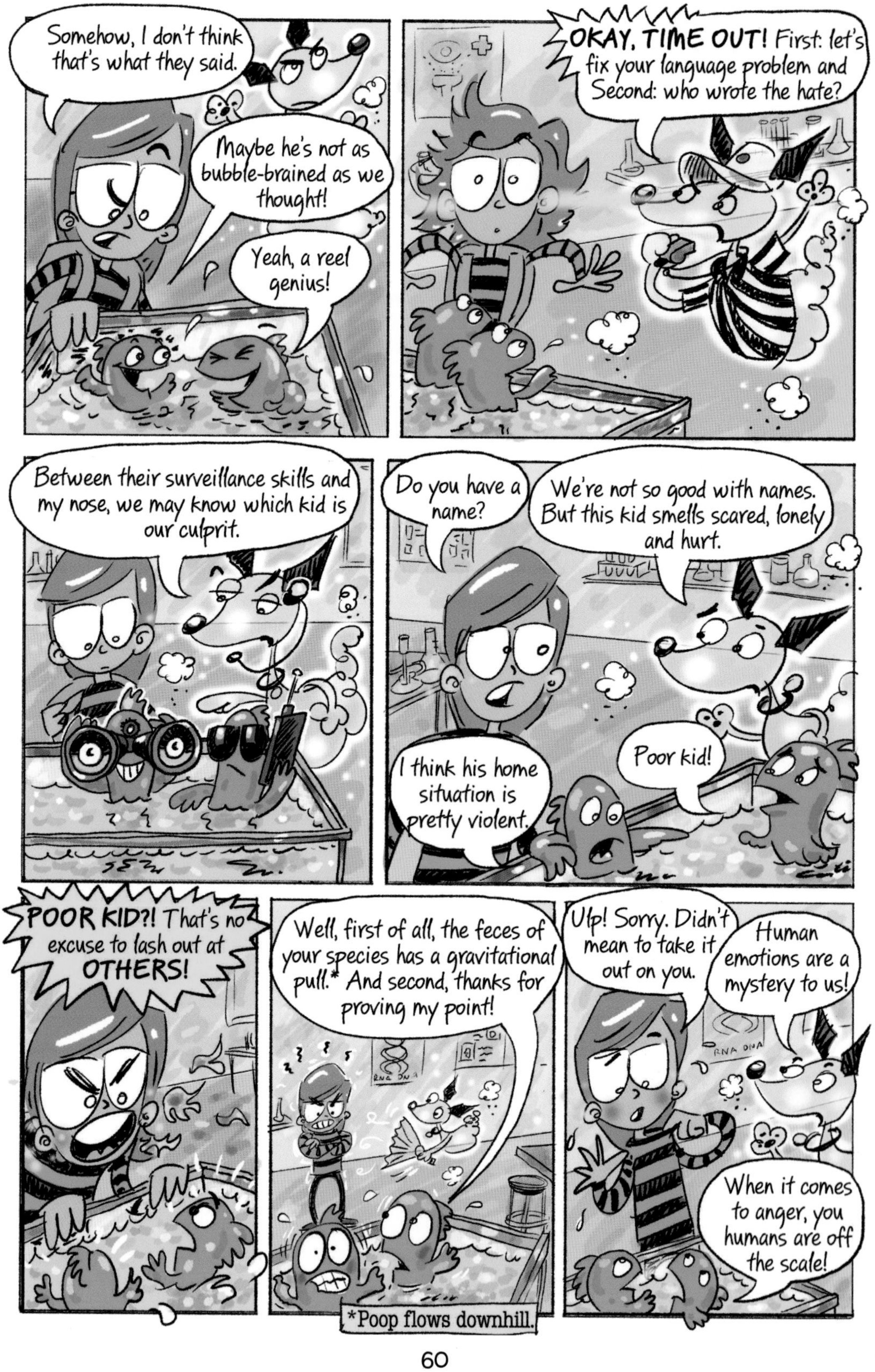
Somehow, I don't think that's what they said.
Maybe he's not as bubble-brained as we thought!
Yeah, a reel genius!
OKAY, TIME OUT! First: let's fix your language problem and Second: who wrote the hate?
Between their surveillance skills and my nose, we may know which kid is our culprit.
Do you have a name?
We're not so good with names. But this kid smells scared, lonely and hurt.
I think his home situation is pretty violent.
Poor kid!
POOR KID?! That's no excuse to lash out at OTHERS!
Well, first of all, the feces of your species has a gravitational pull.* And second, thanks for proving my point!
Ulp! Sorry. Didn't mean to take it out on you.
Human emotions are a mystery to us!
When it comes to anger, you humans are off the scale!
RNA DNA

*Poop flows downhill.

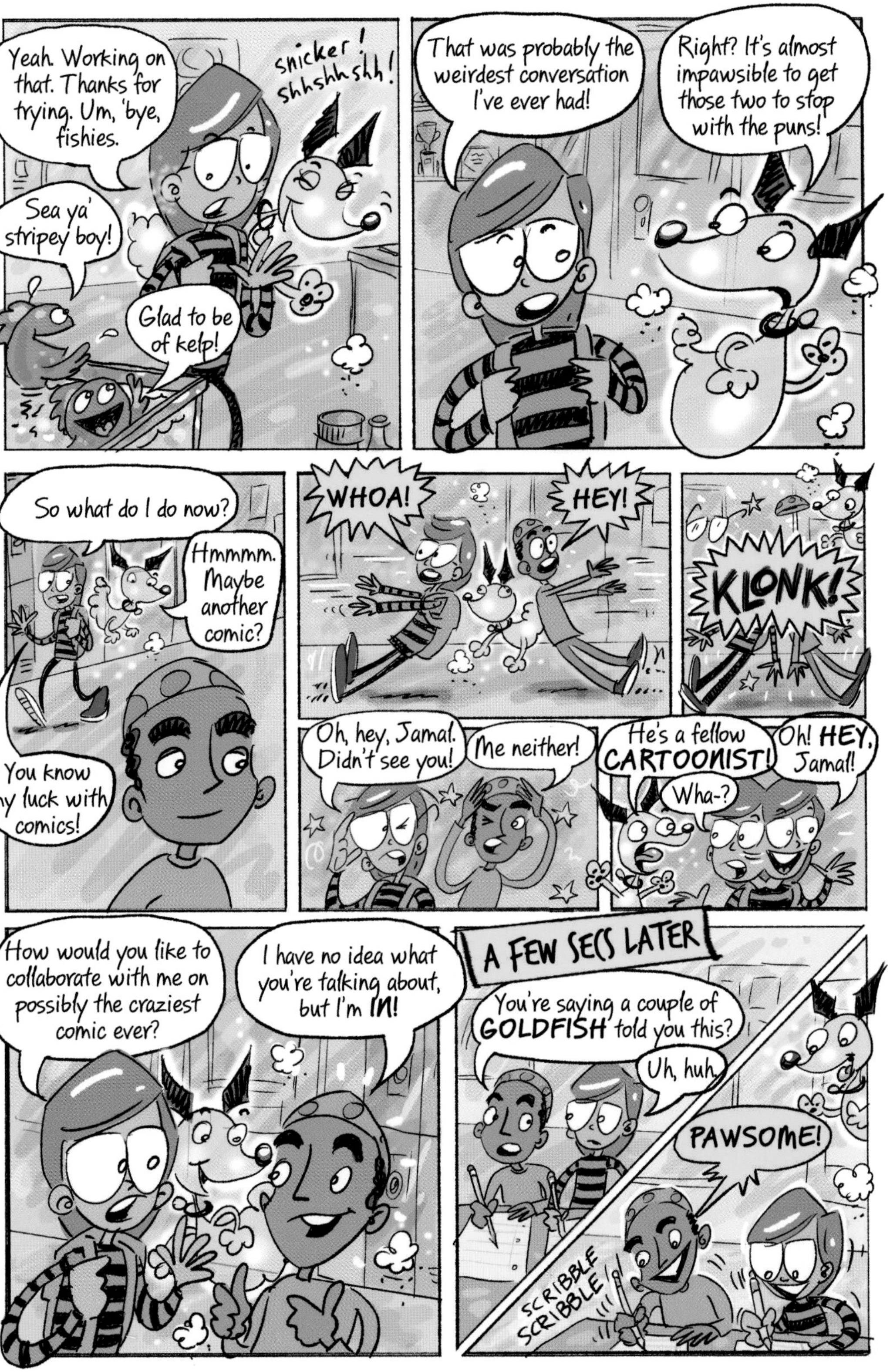
Yeah. Working on that. Thanks for trying. Um, 'bye, fishies.
snicker! shhshhshh!
Sea ya' stripey boy!
Glad to be of kelp!
That was probably the weirdest conversation I've ever had!
Right? It's almost impawsible to get those two to stop with the puns!
So what do I do now?
Hmmmm. Maybe another comic?
You know my luck with comics!
WHOA!
HEY!
KLONK!
Oh, hey, Jamal. Didn't see you!
Me neither!
He's a fellow CARTOONIST!
Oh! HEY, Jamal!
Wha-?
How would you like to collaborate with me on possibly the craziest comic ever?
I have no idea what you're talking about, but I'm IN!
A FEW SECS LATER
You're saying a couple of GOLDFISH told you this?
Uh, huh.
PAWSOME!
SCRIBBLE SCRIBBLE

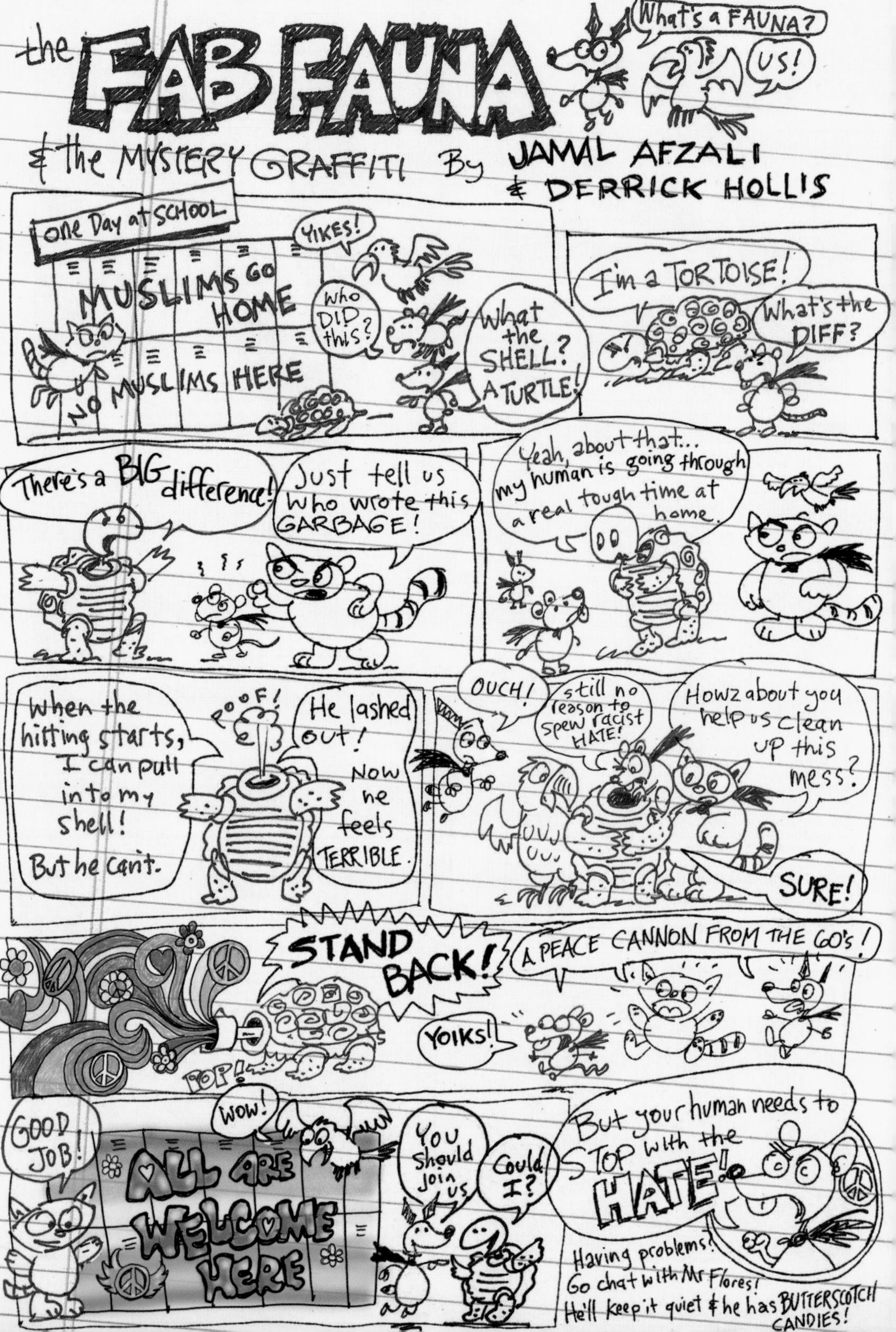
the FAB FAUNA
What's a FAUNA?
US!
& the MYSTERY GRAFFITI By JAMAL AFZALI & DERRICK HOLLIS
One Day at SCHOOL
MUSLIMS GO HOME
NO MUSLIMS HERE
YIKES!
Who DID this?
What the SHELL? A TURTLE!
I'm a TORTOISE!
What's the DIFF?
There's a BIG difference!
Just tell us who wrote this GARBAGE!
Yeah, about that... my human is going through a real tough time at home.
When the hitting starts, I can pull into my shell!
But he can't.
POOF!
He lashed out!
Now he feels TERRIBLE.
OUCH!
still no reason to spew racist HATE!
Howz about you help us clean up this mess?
SURE!
STAND BACK!
A PEACE CANNON FROM THE 60's!
YOIKS!
POP!
GOOD JOB!
WOW!
ALL ARE WELCOME HERE
YOU should join us
Could I?
But your human needs to STOP with the HATE!
Having problems? Go chat with Mr Flores! He'll keep it quiet & he has BUTTERSCOTCH CANDIES!

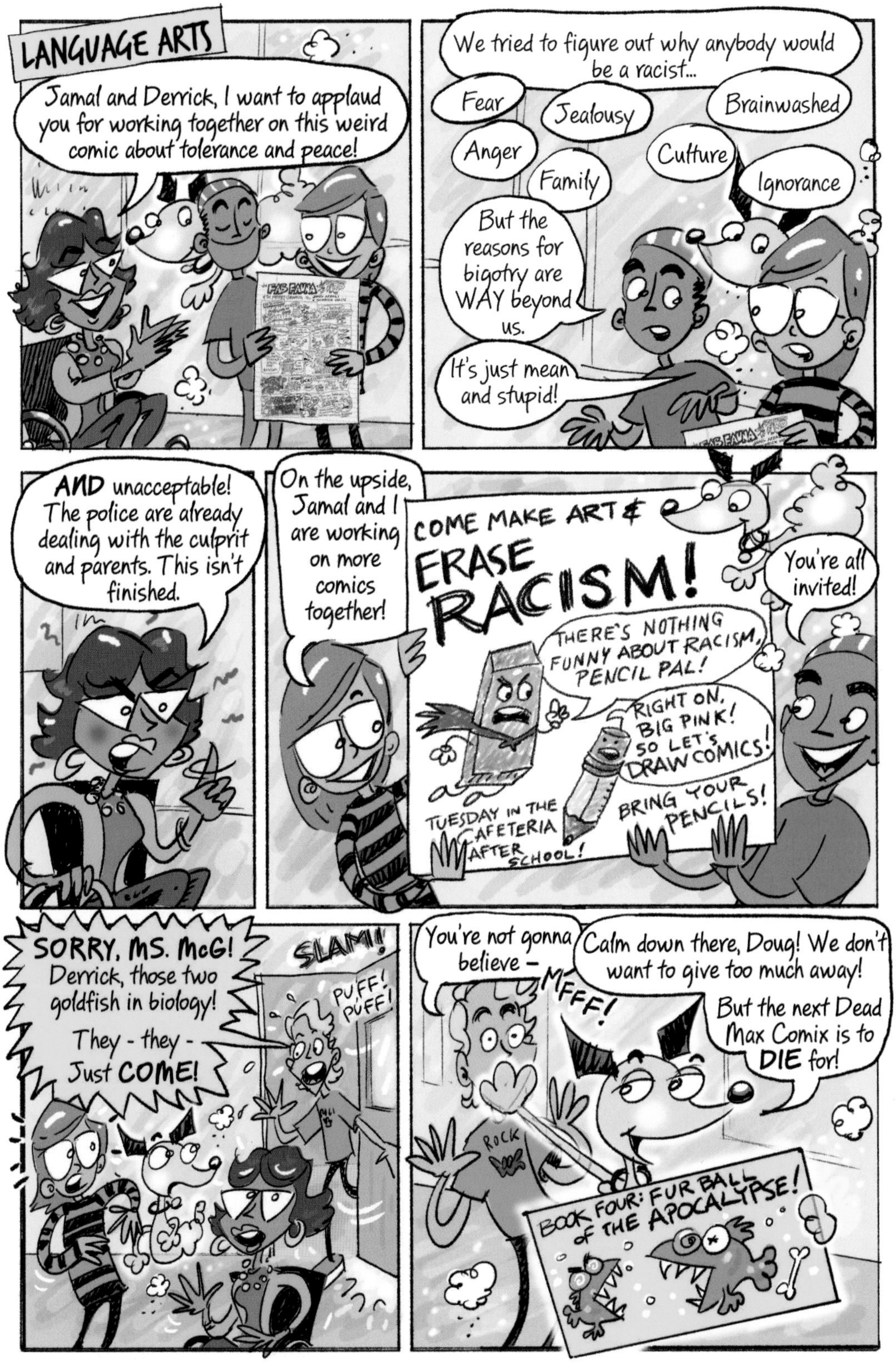
LANGUAGE ARTS
Jamal and Derrick, I want to applaud you for working together on this weird comic about tolerance and peace!
We tried to figure out why anybody would be a racist...
Fear
Jealousy
Brainwashed
Anger
Family
Culture
Ignorance
But the reasons for bigotry are WAY beyond us.
It's just mean and stupid!
AND unacceptable! The police are already dealing with the culprit and parents. This isn't finished.
On the upside, Jamal and I are working on more comics together!
COME MAKE ART &
ERASE RACISM!
THERE'S NOTHING FUNNY ABOUT RACISM, PENCIL PAL!
RIGHT ON, BIG PINK! SO LET'S DRAW COMICS!
TUESDAY IN THE CAFETERIA AFTER SCHOOL!
BRING YOUR PENCILS!
You're all invited!
SORRY, MS. McG! Derrick, those two goldfish in biology!
They - they - Just COME!
SLAM!
PUFF! PUFF!
You're not gonna believe —
MFFF!
Calm down there, Doug! We don't want to give too much away!
But the next Dead Max Comix is to DIE for!
ROCK
BOOK FOUR: FUR BALL OF THE APOCALYPSE!

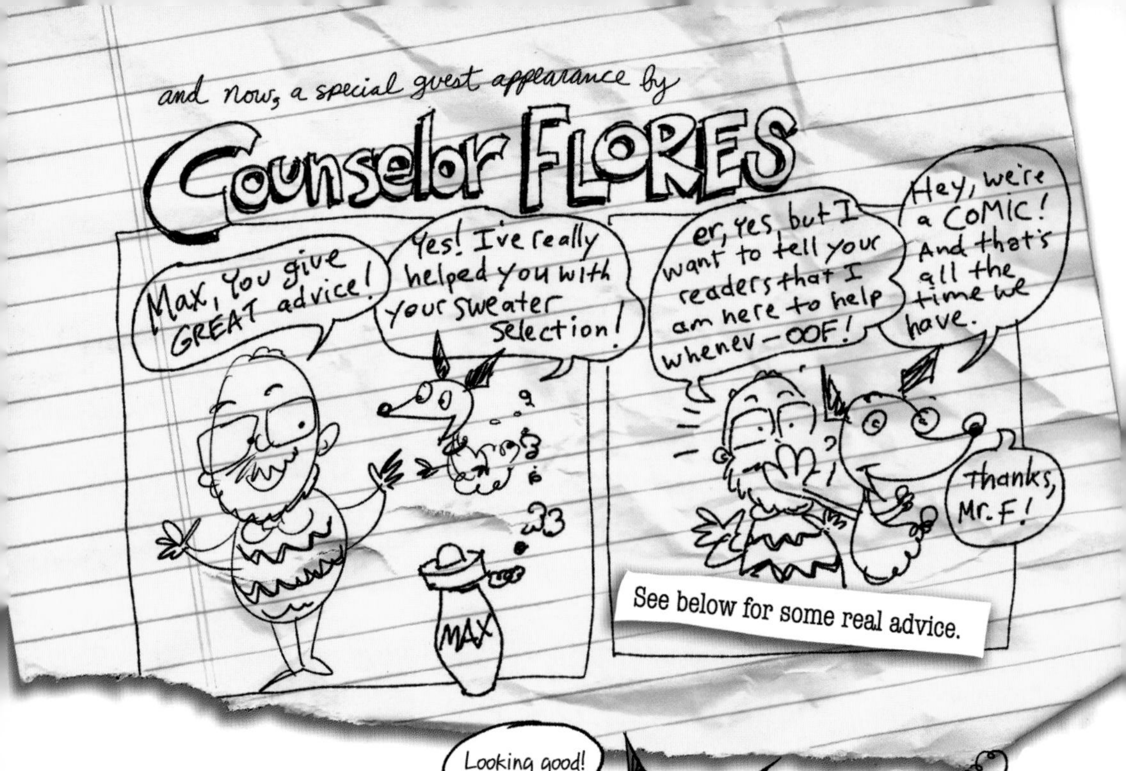
and now, a special guest appearance by
Counselor FLORES
Max, You give GREAT advice!
Yes! I've really helped you with your sweater selection!
MAX
er, yes, but I want to tell your readers that I am here to help whenev—OOF!
Hey, we're a COMIC! And that's all the time we have.
Thanks, Mr. F!
See below for some real advice.

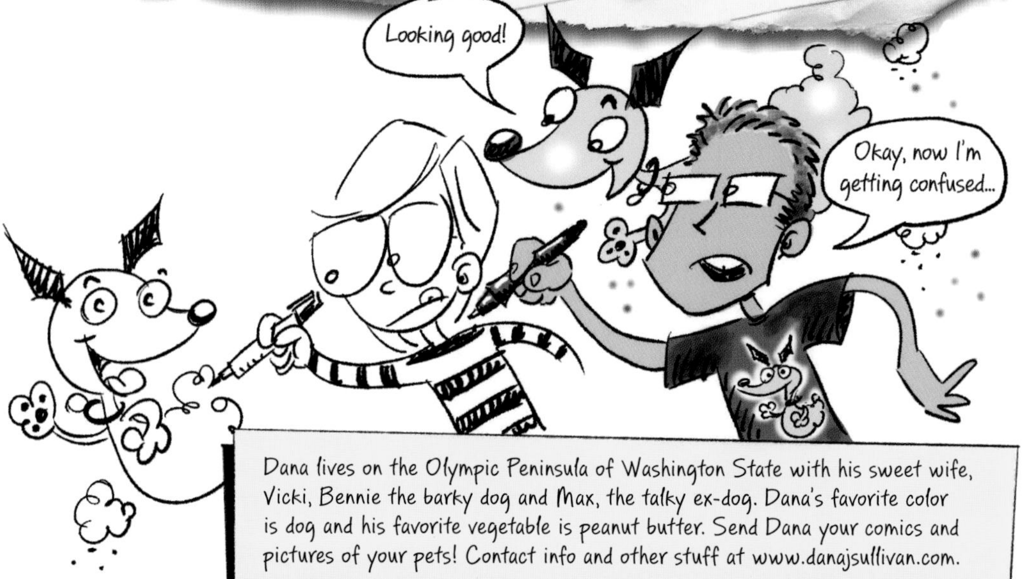
Looking good!
Okay, now I'm getting confused...

Dana lives on the Olympic Peninsula of Washington State with his sweet wife, Vicki, Bennie the barky dog and Max, the talky ex-dog. Dana's favorite color is dog and his favorite vegetable is peanut butter. Send Dana your comics and pictures of your pets! Contact info and other stuff at www.danajsullivan.com.

Max is one smart ex-dog, but, as Counselor Flores says, sometimes it's good to talk to a human. Your school counselor is a great person to start with. They got into this biz because they **WANT** to help kids! Here's some online help too:

For bullying, go to www.stopbullying.gov and click on the "What Kids Can Do" link. And for general, "what's going on with me?" stuff: here are two excellent confidential resources:
Crisis Text Line: 741-741 (USA) or 686868 (Canada) to connect with an online volunteer
National Suicide Prevention Lifeline: 1-800-273-TALK (8255) suicidepreventionlifeline.org
And please know this: **YOU ARE NOT ALONE!** We all need some help from time to time.

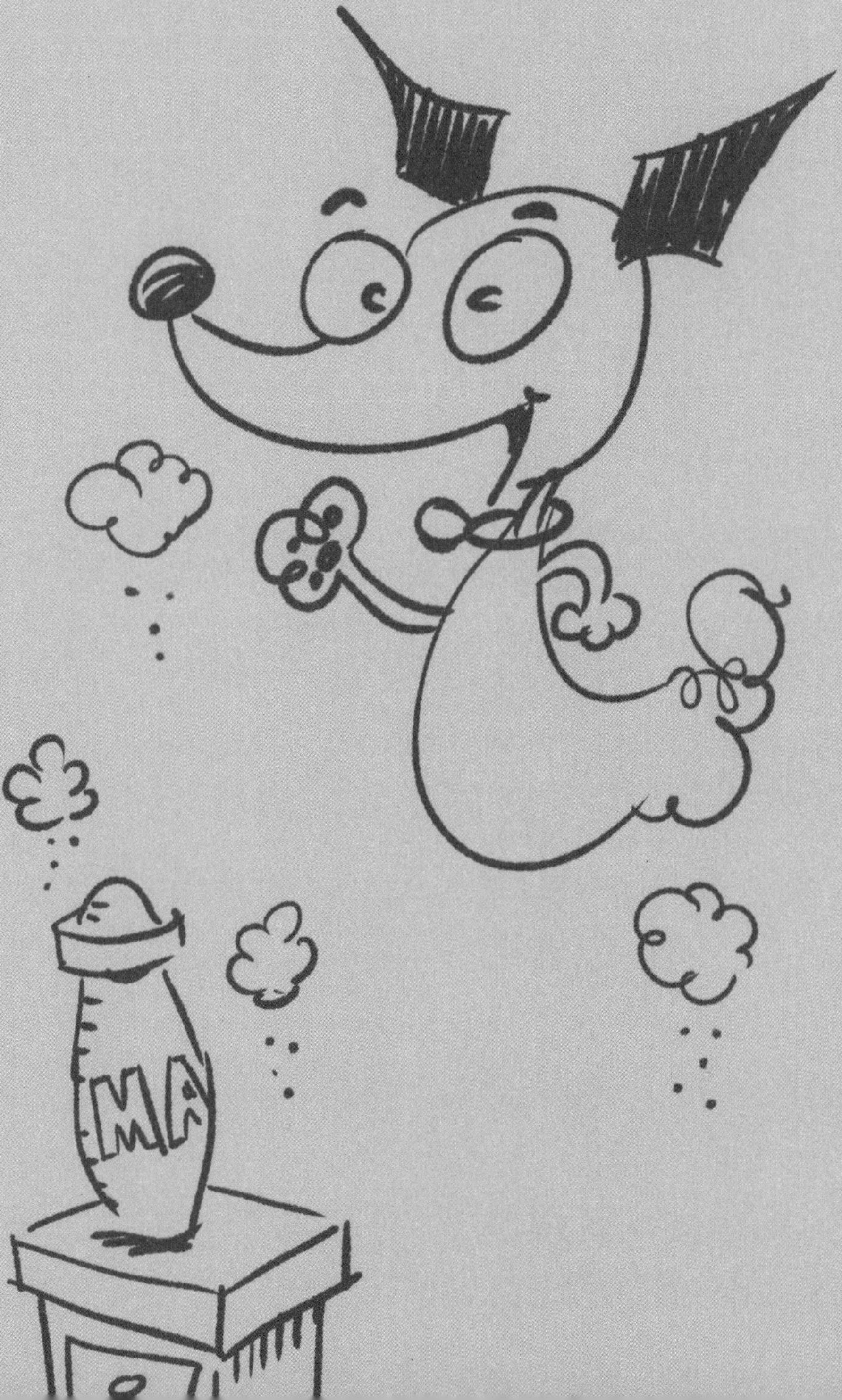
MA

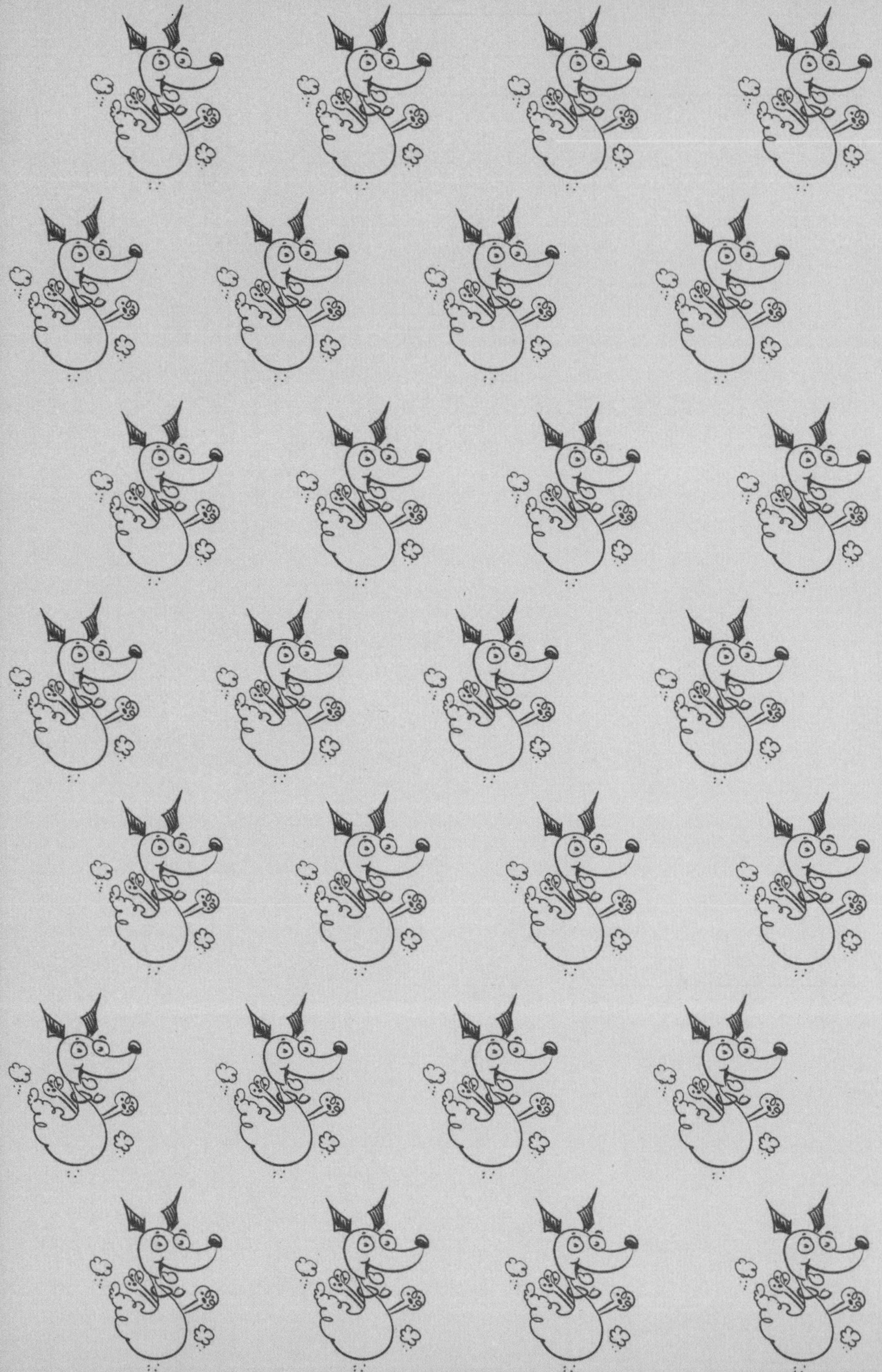